One in a Million

Also by
Kimberla Lawson Roby

One in
a Million

Kimberla Lawson Roby

wm

WILLIAM MORROW
An Imprint of HarperCollins*Publishers*

This book is a work of fiction. The characters, incidents, and dialogue are drawn from the author's imagination and are not to be construed as real. Any resemblance to actual events or persons, living or dead, is entirely coincidental.

HarperCollins books may be purchased for educational, business, or sales promotional use. For information please write: Special Markets Department, HarperCollins Publishers, 10 East 53rd Street, New York, NY 10022.

FIRST EDITION

Designed by Kate Nichols

Library of Congress Cataloging-in-Publication Data

Roby, Kimberla Lawson.
    One in a million / Kimberla Lawson Roby. — 1st ed.
        p. cm.
    ISBN 978-0-06-144295-7
        1. African Americans—Fiction. 2. Spouses—Fiction. I. Title.

PS3568.03189054 2008
813'.54—dc22   2007040690

08 09 10 11 12   OV/RRD   10 9 8 7 6 5 4 3 2 1

For Dr. Betty Price

A wonderfully compassionate woman—
a woman who has shown me and so
many others such genuine love

Acknowledgments

As always, I am thankful to God for all Your love and the many blessings You have so graciously given me; my husband, Will, the love of my life, for all that you are and for always believing in me no matter what; my brothers, Willie and Michael; my stepson and daughter-in-law, Trenod and Tasha, and the rest of my family members for all of your unwavering and continued love and support; and to my friends, my girls, my sisters—Kelli, Lori, and Janell—for everything.

To my very talented and very hardworking assistant, Connie Dettman, the woman I was blessed to connect with right when *Love and Lies* was first released: When I say you were sent from God, I really do mean exactly that. You have made my working life so much more manageable, and I appreciate all that you do for me daily.

Thank you to my agent, Elaine Koster, for everything and then some; to my fabulous and very caring Harper/Morrow/

Avon team (or as my publisher, Lisa G., would say, "Team Roby," which she is so very right about!): Carolyn Marino, Lisa Gallagher, Pamela Spengler-Jaffee, Ben Bruton, Debbie Stier, Tavia Kowalchuk, Lynn Grady, Wendy Lee, Lauren Manzella, Richard Aquan, Buzzy Porter, Michael Morris, and Mike Spradlin, to name a few, and of course to everyone else at Morrow/Avon who works so tirelessly on promoting and distributing my books. What you do for me means the world, and I will never be able to thank you enough.

Thank you to my wonderful church family at Providence Missionary Baptist Church, for all the love and support you have shown me my entire life; and to Dr. Betty Price, Dr. Fred, and the Price daughters, Angela, Cheryl, and Stephanie, for always welcoming Will and me at Crenshaw Christian Center with such open arms.

To the amazing book club discussion groups, bookstores, retailers, and libraries that host my events throughout every year and to all the print, radio, and television media outlets and personalities, both locally and nationally, who are kind enough to publicize my work, thank you.

To my loyal and very compassionate readers who encourage me to write one book after another: I certainly couldn't do this without every one of you, and for that I am beyond grateful.

Much love and God bless,

Kimberla Lawson Roby

Chapter 1

Kennedi sat on the family room sofa, completely in a daze. This just couldn't be, was all she could think. Of course, she'd only learned the incredible news less than thirty minutes ago, but still, it just wasn't sinking in the way she needed it to. It didn't seem real, and the more she replayed the entire scenario, over and over, the more it felt like some fantasy—like some crazy dream her subconscious had concocted.

She was trying her best to accept what she now knew had to be the truth, but she wasn't sure how to deal with it. She wasn't sure what her next steps should be, although she guessed the first thing she needed to do was call her husband, Blake, on his cell phone. There was no doubt he'd be just as stunned as she was, and she couldn't imagine telling anyone else before telling him, not when this was the one thing he'd been hoping for ever since they married ten years ago.

Kennedi hurried into the kitchen, picked up the cordless

phone, and dialed Blake's number. It rang four times before going into voice mail, and she wondered why he wasn't answering. He'd left for the health club more than two hours ago, but normally he only worked out for about an hour, meaning he should have been on his way home by now.

Still, she left him a brief message.

"Hi, honey, it's me. I have something really, really important to tell you, so call me as soon as you get this, okay? Love you."

She ended the call but took the phone with her and headed back into the family room. She hoped he would return her call pretty quickly, because for some reason, she was finally starting to feel truly excited. She was starting to feel a lot happier as the seconds passed, and now she couldn't wait to tell him everything. As a matter of fact, she was now so blissfully beside herself and so dying to tell someone that she considered calling her best friend, Patrice. And she would have, except she knew Blake would be livid if he learned he hadn't been told first, so instead, she dialed his number again, and again, and again. However, it was all to no avail, and she was starting to get worried. Either that or her nerves were simply getting the best of her. She wasn't sure which it was, but she knew she needed to try to calm down. She needed to focus on something totally unrelated to this remarkable news she suddenly couldn't stop smiling about.

Kennedi walked back into the kitchen again, pulled a glass from the cupboard, pressed it against the ice dispenser inside the refrigerator door until seven or eight cubes fell inside, and then set it down on the granite island. Next she opened the refrigerator, removed a pitcher of red grapefruit Crystal Light, and filled her glass to the brim. She loved this flavor, and besides the FDA's recommended eight glasses of water a day, she hardly drank anything else. She did have an occasional caffeine-free soda every now and then, but never more than a couple times per month, thanks to the pact she and her mom had made a few years ago. They'd both agreed to forgo caffeinated drinks altogether and to drink carbonated drinks only once in a while, but this was after her mom had been diagnosed with breast cancer and Kennedi had read an article stating that caffeine had been suggested as a possible risk factor for her mom's illness. Needless to say, her mom had given up her daily before-work vanilla latte from Starbucks almost immediately, and unlike Kennedi, she'd even given up drinks that contained artificial sweeteners. She'd quickly begun taking every precaution she could, trying her best to combat the horrible disease that was attacking her.

But sadly, in the end, none of her new health-conscious efforts, the removal of both of her breasts, chemotherapy, or radiation had been enough. The doctors had done all they could do, and actually, for about a year or more she'd remained in remission. That is, until six months ago, when she'd slipped back out of it and then passed away three months later.

Now Kennedi was looking through the patio doors in tears. She wasn't weeping uncontrollably, the way she had the entire first month after her mom's funeral, but right now she would have done anything, anything at all, to see her mother again. She'd have done anything to have her back with her, even if only for a short while, because she missed her terribly. She missed the woman who would have given her last dollar if it meant helping someone else.

Although, as an only child, Kennedi couldn't thank God enough for allowing her the chance to take care of her mom. At first, she hadn't known what she was going to do, but Blake had made it clear that it was more than okay for her to take a leave of absence from work so she could spend as much time with her mom as possible. Needless to say, this was exactly what Kennedi had been hoping she could do, but she'd worried about their finances. She'd worried that, for the first time since they'd gotten married, they wouldn't be able to pay their bills on time. But Blake had promised her they would be fine. He'd told her that they wouldn't be able to spend money on unnecessary items, but that they also wouldn't end up with credit problems either. He'd told her that he loved his mother-in-law no differently than if she'd been his own mother and that allowing Kennedi to take a leave without pay was the very least he could do. He'd insisted that living without two incomes was a sacrifice he had no problem making, and Kennedi loved him so much for what he'd done. She loved him because not every husband would have made such a loving and very selfless offer.

Kennedi wiped the wetness from both sides of her face but the tears kept flowing. Oh how she wished her mom was still there so she could witness the blessing she and Blake were about to have bestowed upon them. She could practically hear her mother screaming with great joy, and what comforted Kennedi was the fact that her mother would always remain cozily in her heart, that her soul was alive and well, and that knowing her, she was probably already moseying around in heaven, telling everyone who would listen about the good news.

Kennedi sniffled and wiped her eyes, but then she smiled when she saw the door opening. She hadn't even heard Blake drive into the garage, probably because she'd been so consumed with thoughts of her mother, but she was so glad he'd finally made it home.

"Why didn't you call me back?" she asked, walking toward her tall, muscular, exceptionally handsome husband.

"Actually, I didn't even think to check my phone."

"Well, you need to sit down for this one, because you'll never believe what I have to tell you. It's the best news ever."

"That's fine, but there's something I need to tell you first."

"But this can't wait," she declared excitedly.

"Kennedi, please," he said, locking both his hands together in front of his chest. "Please, just sit down before I lose my nerve."

Kennedi didn't like the sound of his voice or the look on his face, and suddenly he was scaring her. "Blake, what is it?"

He sat down at the island, across from where she was standing. "Please, just have a seat."

This time, Kennedi did what he asked. She gave him her undivided attention, but Blake sighed pretty loudly.

"It's taken me two weeks just to build up enough courage to do this, and I just can't delay it any longer. I've waited too long as it is."

Kennedi tried to stay positive, but she didn't know what she was going to do if something was wrong with Blake. He'd gone for his yearly physical maybe a month ago, and now she worried that when he'd told her all of his lab results were fine, he hadn't told her the truth. She worried that some major illness had struck him and that she was about to lose him.

Blake looked at her and then sighed again. "Okay, the thing is this. I haven't loved you for almost two years now, I've been seeing someone else the entire time, I'm in love with her, and . . . I want a divorce."

Kennedi stared at Blake in a staggered yet deranged sort of

way. She did this because, clearly, there was no way she'd heard him correctly. "What did you say?"

"I don't love you anymore, I haven't for a long time, and I want a divorce."

These particular words were a bit different from the words he'd spoken the first time around—at least she thought they were—but still, they basically meant the same thing. They meant he wanted out of the marriage and wanted nothing more to do with her. And had he truly said he'd been seeing someone else for almost two years?

"Kennedi, I'm really, really sorry about this," she heard him say, but the rest of what he said was a total blur. She could hear him speaking, but she couldn't make out what he was actually saying. It was as if she'd entered into oblivion and couldn't snap herself out of it.

But then she heard her name being called repeatedly and realized she'd only been dreaming. She realized that she'd merely been having a nightmare, and she was glad it was over with.

"I'm hoping we can handle all of this like two mature adults, because it'll make the entire process a whole lot easier."

Oh my God, Kennedi thought. She hadn't been dreaming at all, and Blake seemed more serious now than she'd ever seen him.

"Who is she?" Kennedi finally asked, her heart beating rapidly.

"I don't think that really matters."

"And why is that?"

"Because it just doesn't."

"Well, it does to me. As a matter of fact, I think it matters a whole lot."

"I disagree. Especially since she has nothing to do with our situation."

Kennedi frowned. "Excuse me?"

"Look, I've told you how I feel, and if it's any consolation, I didn't go looking for this. It was never my plan to have an affair, but once it started, I couldn't stop it. I tried, but the more time went on, the more I fell in love with her."

"I don't believe this is happening."

"In all honesty, I wanted to tell you a few months ago."

"Oh really? And is there some great reason why you didn't?"

"Yes. Your mom."

"My mom knew about this?" Kennedi said, raising her voice.

"No. Of course not. But when the doctors gave her only a few months to live, I just couldn't burden you with all of this. I knew she was going to die, and I figured it was best if I just waited until afterward."

"Well, how wonderfully considerate of you."

"There's something else you should know," he pronounced without delay.

"And what is that?"

"I'm moving out this evening."

Kennedi's heart skipped a beat, and her body went numb.

"I'm sorry, but I'm now at the point where I can't stand being without her."

"Wow. This is totally and ridiculously inconceivable. I mean, I just can't believe you're doing this. Not after all the years we've been together. Not after all the love we've shared since the day we met."

"I'm sorry."

"Will you stop saying that!" Kennedi screamed, and then stood up.

"Fine," he said, and then got up himself. "If that's the way you want it. Fine."

"It is, because the more you keep apologizing, the more disgusted I'm becoming. The more I want to pay you back in a way I'll surely end up regretting."

Blake looked at her for more than a few seconds and shook his head. "I think it's best that I just get my things and go."

Kennedi gazed at him in silence, and he finally left the room. But when he did, all she could think about was how he'd never even given her the chance to tell him her good news. He'd never given her one opportunity to tell him that yesterday, she'd played the multistate Mega Millions game . . . that today she'd checked the newspaper . . . and learned she had every single number.

He'd never given her a chance to tell him that this week's jackpot was fifty million dollars.

Chapter 2

Kennedi opened her eyes, glanced over at the digital clock radio, and then looked toward the textured ceiling. It was seven A.M., only twenty minutes since the last time she'd awakened and checked to see what time it was, and she was terribly exhausted. Blake had packed a couple of suitcases and a garment bag and hadn't said a word until he was ready to leave for good; even then, all he'd told her was that he'd be back for the rest of his things this weekend. Kennedi had wanted to talk to him, and as foolish as it probably sounded, she'd wanted to beg him not to leave her, not after what she'd considered ten wonderful years of marriage, but instead, she hadn't said a word. What she'd done was watch him, from the upstairs window, backing his Cadillac SUV out of the driveway, and then she'd tossed and turned and cried her eyes out until the wee hours of this morning.

Now she lay there wondering how she'd arrived at such a

horrible place in her life. She wondered what she could have done differently and, more important, how she could have been a better wife to Blake. She wondered when he'd fallen out of love with her and in love with another woman. He'd claimed that this had all occurred about two years ago, but Kennedi wanted to know exactly when. She wanted to know when and where he'd met her, the first time they'd officially spent time together, the first time they'd had sex. She wanted to know all the specifics of this wicked affair Blake had gotten himself caught up in, and she wanted to know who this home wrecker was. Not that any of this information was going to make Kennedi feel any better, but her curiosity was starting to consume her and she couldn't think about anything else, not even the lottery jackpot she'd soon be the recipient of.

Kennedi finally dragged herself out of bed and into the bathroom. Once there, she stood in front of the vanity, turned on the faucet, and waited for it to heat up. Then she gazed into the mirror at her scattered shoulder-length hair and broke into tears all over again. She stood there for a few minutes, trying to settle her emotions, and then she turned off the water and went back into the bedroom. There was no way she'd be able to face any of her coworkers today, so she sat down and dialed her supervisor's direct number. As usual, he was already in his office.

"This is Carson speaking."

"Hi, Carson, this is Kennedi."

"Hey, you don't sound too well, is everything okay?"

"Not really, but I'll be fine. I was wondering, though, if you'd have a problem with me taking a personal day today."

"Not at all. We don't have a lot going until next week, so I think the rest of us can hold down the fort while you're gone."

His voice was cheerful, and Kennedi always appreciated that about him.

"Thanks so much for understanding, and I'll see you tomorrow."

"You take care of yourself."

With the exception of the three-month leave of absence she'd taken to spend time with her mother, she'd rarely missed any days of work the whole five years she'd been employed with Travis-Martin International. She'd been hired in as a human resources specialist, and her boss, Carson, who was director, had all but promised that she'd be the next human resources manager for salaried employees. She'd loved her job and the people she worked with from the very beginning, and it saddened her to know that she probably wouldn't be seeing them on a regular basis much longer, not with her coming into millions of dollars the way she was. But at the moment, she didn't want to think about any of that. She couldn't think about it, because no matter how wealthy she was going to be, somehow it no longer meant as much as it had yesterday, now that she knew her marriage was basically over. It didn't matter as much because what good was money or any other luxury if you had no one special to share it with?

Kennedi went back into the bathroom; cleansed, toned, and moisturized her face; brushed her teeth; and rinsed with mouthwash. Then she slipped out of her satin nightgown—the one Blake had given her four months ago on Valentine's Day—laid it across the brass towel rack, and turned on the shower. But before she stepped inside, she looked back at the gown and wondered why Blake would have given her such a beautifully romantic gift if he was so in love with someone else. She wondered how he'd been able to keep a straight face whenever he was there at home with her, knowing that he was seeing someone else behind her back. She wondered how he could betray her in such a ruthless way, yet still make love to her as recently as this past weekend. It was true that their level of intimacy had changed over the last couple of years and that they only had sex once or twice per week, but Kennedi never would have guessed that Blake was having an affair. She never would have guessed that he was sleeping with two women at the same time. . . .

"Oh, dear God, no," she said out loud, and then covered her mouth with both hands. She'd been so shocked and upset about Blake's adultery and his decision to leave her that she hadn't even considered the fact that her health and possibly her life might be in danger. She'd never even taken the time to think about the fact that Blake might have been having unprotected sex with this woman like it was nothing. Men did careless crap such as this all the time, and the idea that he might have contracted some deadly virus, particularly one called HIV, was enough to send Kennedi into a frenzy. It was enough to send warm chills, if there was such a thing, through her entire body, and she knew she had to get tested. She knew she had to visit her doctor's office, no matter how humiliating this was all going to be. She could kill Blake for placing her in this position.

About a half hour after she'd gotten dressed, Kennedi decided it was time she called Patrice. She'd wanted to phone her last night, right after Blake had left, but even though Patrice was her best friend and actually more like a sister to her, she hadn't been in any shape to talk to anyone. She'd been much too devastated and, for the most part, speechless.

Kennedi dialed Patrice's number, placed the phone between her ear and shoulder, and rubbed shea butter on her hands.

"Hey, girl," Patrice said. "And why are you calling me from home? Why aren't you at work? Because I know little miss I-don't-play-hooky-from-work-no-matter-what isn't doing exactly that, now are you?"

"P, you have no idea how I wish that was my real reason for not going in today. You have no idea at all."

"Why? What's wrong?"

"Can you come over?"

"This sounds serious."

"It is."

"I was going to make a couple of calls to two of my clients, but if you really need me, it can wait until later this afternoon."

"If you don't mind, I sure would appreciate it, because I really need you right now."

"Kennedi, you're worrying me, girl, so please tell me what's going on. I'll be over as soon as I get dressed, but you have to at least tell me what's got you so upset, because I can hear it in your voice."

"Blake moved out last night."

"He what?!"

"He left and he's not coming back."

"I'll be there within the hour," Patrice said, and hung up.

What I want to know is who this tramp is," Patrice said after Kennedi told her everything. They'd been sitting in the kitchen for a few minutes, but now Patrice was up walking around and making threatening hand movements. She was more livid than Kennedi had expected her to be.

"He wouldn't say."

"Well, that's beside the point, because we'll find out soon enough, anyway."

"I still can't believe this is happening. I mean, no matter how much I keep playing Blake's words over and over, it just doesn't make any sense."

"I can only imagine, because I don't get it either. I've known Blake from the time you and him started dating, and he's the last man on this earth I would have suspected to be cheating."

"Yeah, which just goes to show you can't trust anyone. You can't trust anyone at all."

"That's probably true, for the most part anyway, but Kennedi, I hope you know you can trust me. Always."

"I do know that, but when it comes to men, I don't know if I'll ever be able to trust another one again. Not after this. Not after being in love with the same person all these years, thinking he felt the same way about me, but then hearing that he doesn't and hasn't for a long time."

"These women out here are something else, because while Blake is completely at fault, this woman knew he was married and she never should have even considered having a relationship with him."

"You and I know that, but not every woman feels the way we do. Not every woman has strong moral values, and a lot of them couldn't care less about the vows a man has taken with his wife before God. Women who sleep with married men basically have no conscience, and they are no better than dogs living on the street."

"You're right, but it has never occurred to me to take up with any man who belongs to someone else. Not ever. Not now at thirty-nine and not even when I was in my twenties."

Kennedi sighed. "Neither have I, but . . ."

"Blake should be ashamed of himself, and I can't tell you how disappointed I am in him. Not to mention how outraged I am because of what he's done to you."

"Well, actually, that wasn't the only startling news I received yesterday."

"After what you've already told me, I don't even know if I want to hear it."

"It's not bad."

"Good."

"You're not going to believe it, but I had all the numbers that were drawn for the Mega Millions game two nights ago."

Patrice cracked up laughing.

"I told you you wouldn't believe it, but it's true."

"You are too much," Patrice said, still chuckling. "But I have to say that I think it's wonderful how you're not letting this whole mess with Blake get you down and that you're still able to joke around and have some fun."

"P, it's no joke. I've never been more serious about anything. I'm really telling you the truth."

"Will you stop that?" Patrice told her, now laughing harder than before.

But then Kennedi reached into her purse and pulled out both the ticket and the local section of the newspaper. "Here."

Patrice took each item into her hands, looking at the newspaper first and then at the ticket. Then she looked at Kennedi. But apparently she still couldn't fathom it, because she scanned everything again. Then she set the paper and the ticket down on the island. "This is mad crazy."

"Isn't it though?"

"Oh my goodness. You actually won the entire jackpot."

"I know, and what are the chances of that happening?"

"They're next to none, but you sure don't sound too excited. I mean, I don't even know how you can sit there all nonchalant the way you are. You ought to be jumping toward the moon."

"It's hard to feel happy and excited about something when you've had your whole world turned upside-down."

"I guess it would be sort of bittersweet for me, too, if I were you. But I can't get over this. As a matter of fact, I was just watching the news last night and heard one of the anchors saying that there was only one winner this week and that the ticket had been purchased here in Covington Park, but I never would have thought in a million years that they were talking about you. They were also saying that the person hadn't come forward and that so many people had played on the day of the drawing that the pot ended up totaling out at around sixty-three million."

"Are you kidding? Because it was around fifty when I bought the ticket."

"No. I'm positive."

"Wow."

"Wow is right, but you've got to get this taken care of. I know you're hurting, but girl, you've got to put that aside for the time being."

"I know, and that's why I've already called my attorney and made an appointment for this afternoon. I didn't tell him why, but I explained that it was an urgent matter."

"Good. And what about your accountant?"

"I was going to call him first, but then I remembered that he and Blake have gone golfing together a few times, and the last thing I want is for Blake to find out about this. So I asked my attorney to bring in one of the accountants they do a lot of business with."

"You don't think Blake would have the audacity to try and claim some of the money, do you? I mean, he wouldn't dare after slithering in here like the snake he is and then proclaiming his undying love for some whore."

"I don't know, but I wouldn't put it past him, and I'll just have to deal with that when and if the time comes."

"I guess so. But hey, I just have to ask you this. What in the world possessed you to even buy that ticket? Because for as long as I can remember, Blake has always been the *only* lottery player in this household."

"Tell me about it. With the exception of a few times over the years when Blake would practically beg me to play, you know I've never believed in throwing away any of my hard-earned money to the lottery. But the other day, I just so happened to run into the convenience store, and I heard this couple going on and on about what they were going to do with all this money after they won it. We sort of chatted and laughed about it, and then I thought, 'Why not?' Especially since Blake has always believed he was going to hit it big. To be honest, I was pretty much just doing something to be doing it, and I never expected to win one dime."

"Well, you did, and I couldn't be happier for you. I mean, really, Kennedi, I know gambling sort of goes against what we believe as Christians, but it couldn't have happened to a better person. You deserve this."

"Maybe."

"I know this is a tough time for you, but I promise you,

things will get better. And as angry as I am with Blake right now, who's to say he won't come to his senses? Who's to say that he won't eventually realize what a huge mistake he made and that he's given up the best thing that ever happened to him?"

"I don't think so. Not after seeing how strongly he felt about what he was saying to me. Plus, even though I still love him and I'm already missing him so, so much, I don't think I could ever get past this. I really don't think I could ever take him back."

"Well, regardless of what happens, I'm here for you."

"I know that. And Patrice, I'm really depending on it."

Chapter 3

As Patrice turned her Mercedes E350 out of the subdivision, Kennedi was glad Patrice had been able to take off the rest of the afternoon. Of course, it wasn't all that hard to do, what with Patrice working as an independent contractor, consulting for small businesses that needed help with start-up procedures and marketing. Patrice had worked as a marketing manager for a number of years, but when she realized she could double her salary she'd decided to branch out on her own. She'd made the transition two years ago and was already at the point where she had to farm out a number of projects to other contractors because she didn't have time to handle them all on her own. Although Patrice never complained about having to give up any work coming her way, because she always earned a huge percentage from those assignments as well.

"P, thanks again for spending all this time with me, because I know you weren't planning on it."

"Don't waste another thought on that. You are my priority right now and everything else is secondary. You said you wanted me to come with you, and that's all I needed to hear."

Kennedi felt her eyes filling up, but she refused to shed any more tears. She'd been crying on and off for nearly twenty-four hours and enough was enough. At least for the rest of today, anyway. She had business to tend to, and it was time she did what her cousin's teenage son would tell her to do: "man up." It was time she doubled her determination and did whatever she had to do so she could make sound decisions.

Patrice and Kennedi drove for a few minutes in silence, headed to one of the office supply stores, but then Patrice spoke.

"I'm so glad you decided to purchase a new safe, because you just can't take any chances. Not with Blake knowing the combination to the one you already have."

"I know. I sort of doubt that he'll be going into it anytime soon, because all we keep in there are things like our wills, power of attorney documents, insurance policies, and marriage license, but just to be sure, I figured it would be best if I bought one that only I'll have access to."

"Trust me, it's a smart move."

Another twenty seconds or so passed, and then, out of nowhere, that whole affair nightmare hit Kennedi like a massive plane crash. "I am so sorry to keep bringing this up," she said, "but can you believe what Blake has been doing behind my back? And all this time, too."

Patrice sighed. "It's like I told you before, I'm just as surprised as you are."

"I feel so stupid and naïve. Like I'm the biggest fool in history."

"But you're not. Some people are good at being slick, and you can't help that you didn't notice what he was up to. And anyway, it's not like you should have had to be suspicious of your own husband. You never should have had to worry about him messing around, not even remotely."

"Maybe not, but I have to admit that the more I think back over the last year, there were a few signs. None that I would have thought twice about had he not told me he was seeing someone else, but there have definitely been some changes."

"Like?"

"Well, for one thing, he's been working a lot later than usual. Not every day, but more often than not. Then, about a year and a half ago, he all of a sudden decided it was time he got his body back in perfect shape. Which I didn't think was any big issue, because we all start to feel that way when we get older, and I just figured it was because he'd turned forty around then."

"I could see that, because I'm feeling that way myself right now."

"And so am I, and I'm sure it's because we're both turning forty this year ourselves. But the only thing I'm thinking about now is that Blake started acting as though he was obsessed with working out. I mean, he goes to the health club six and sometimes seven days a week. And even when he doesn't do that, he's running two to three miles."

"Amazing. And how typical that he'd want to look better for some mistress."

"But you know what's sad?"

"What's that?"

"From the first day I met Blake, I was foolish enough to believe that we'd be married until death. For whatever reason, I never considered the idea that he would eventually want someone else."

"Blake is so wrong for this."

Kennedi shook her head in bewilderment and peered out of the passenger window. Once again, she wished her mom was here. This time, so she could lie in her arms the way she had when she was a child and sometimes when she was an adult. Without question, she would have given up every dime of that lottery jackpot—she would have done anything in her power and would have made every sacrifice necessary just to be able to touch her beautiful face and see her lovely smile. She would have done anything just to have another five minutes with her.

After picking up the new safe and a few other office supplies that Patrice needed, Kennedi realized they still had a little time before the meeting at her attorney's office, so Patrice suggested they stop at a restaurant for a bite to eat.

"We haven't been to that cute little eatery down here on Maple in a little while, so what about that?" Patrice asked.

"To be honest, I'm not all that hungry."

"But when was the last time you had something?"

"I don't know. I guess yesterday morning."

"Then as far as I'm concerned there's nothing else to talk about."

"So I suppose you're my boss now."

"Exactly."

Kennedi smiled, and after another couple of miles, Patrice pulled into the restaurant's parking lot and they left the vehicle and walked inside. It was shortly after one o'clock, past the lunch rush, but still there were a good number of people sitting at tables. Thankfully, though, the line for ordering wasn't all that long.

"So, what do you want?" Patrice started in immediately.

"I think I'll just have some lemonade."

Patrice looked at her with a "whatever" sort of look and then back toward the woman behind the counter. "We'll have two tuna croissants and two lemonades."

The cashier punched everything in and asked, "Will that be all?"

"Yes."

"Then that'll be $15.76," the woman said, and Patrice passed her a twenty-dollar bill and waited for change. Then they moved down a ways to wait for their number to be called, and as soon as it was, they headed toward the first open booth they could find.

"Hey, why don't we see if there's a table outside on the patio. Especially since the weather is so gorgeous today."

"That's fine," Kennedi said, and couldn't help thinking how she and Blake had come here several times last summer for a quick bite to eat.

"Here's one," Patrice pointed out as soon as they stepped through the doorway, and they each took a seat.

But as soon as they did, Kennedi looked over at one of the tables not too far from them and gasped.

"What?" Patrice said.

But Kennedi was too taken aback to say anything.

"What?" Patrice repeated, and then turned all the way around in her chair. "Oh my God," she said, almost shouting, after seeing Blake stretching his hand toward some slightly attractive yet uncultured-looking woman and holding her hand. "Please tell me he's not already flauntin' that tramp out in public like this."

Kennedi still didn't respond, and just at that moment she and Blake made eye contact. He stared for a few seconds and then looked away, and Kennedi could tell he didn't know what to do.

Patrice, on the other hand, was steaming. "I oughtta go tell him and that streetwalker what I think of both of them and then—" Kennedi didn't let her finish her sentence; she was out of her seat and over at the table without even realizing it.

"So, is this the hooker you're leaving me for? Huh? Is this the piece of trash you've been sleeping with behind my back for—what did you say? Two years?"

"Kennedi, please don't embarrass yourself this way," he said. "You're making a scene, and I think it would be best if you went back to your table."

"Back to my table? So, now you're going to try to dismiss me? Even though you're the one sitting out here with your little weave-wearing whore. The one who obviously can't even afford to get her hair done on a regular basis. The one who clearly doesn't know that her kinky hair doesn't match up with that silky mess she's got plastered all through her head."

"Kennedi, I'm asking you nicely."

"You can ask me any way you want, but I'm not leaving here until I get good and ready. I'm still your wife, remember?"

"Not for long," the tramp commented matter-of-factly.

"Are you talking to me?" Kennedi asked, and Patrice attempted to pull Kennedi away. But Kennedi jerked away from her. "So, are you?" she asked the woman again, but she got no response.

"Kennedi, why don't you leave us alone?" Blake blurted out.

But Kennedi had had enough.

"You make me sick!" she yelled, and then she grabbed Blake's salad plate and flipped it toward his chest. Next, she snatched what looked to be a full glass of flavored tea and poured every ounce of it, ice and all, on top of the woman's head.

"You crazy lunatic!" the woman shrieked, and slid her chair backward.

Blake jumped up. "Okay, Kennedi, that's it. Either you leave or I'm calling the police."

"You can call whomever you want because, sweetheart, this is only the beginning. When I'm finished with you, you'll regret the day you ever met me."

Patrice pulled Kennedi's arm with a lot more force, and this time she didn't resist. This time she followed behind her and back over to where they'd been sitting, but she made a point of looking back at her husband, who was trying to help Miss Thing dry her body off. She watched and had a mind to rush back toward them, but Patrice picked up their handbags and said, "Kennedi, please, let's go."

Kennedi hesitated, but when she saw people staring at her from just about every direction, she did what Patrice told her. She followed her out of the eatery like a good little girl but couldn't wait to get even with Blake. She couldn't wait until he found out about all the money she'd won and how he wasn't getting one dime of it.

She couldn't wait to hear him groveling like some sick animal.

Chapter 4

"Are you okay?" Patrice asked as soon as they sat inside her car.

"I'm fine," Kennedi answered, but knew she was anything but.

"This is all my fault, and I am so sorry. I'm the one who suggested we stop to get something to eat, even though you kept saying you didn't want anything."

"No, this is Blake's fault. Period."

"I really thought he was a better man than this, and I certainly never expected to find him parading his mistress around in public. Not while you and he are still married."

"He's so different. And he's acting like this woman means everything to him."

"Who is she, anyway? And how did he meet her?"

Kennedi had no clue, but she couldn't deny that she was bothered by the fact that Miss Thing looked at least five years younger than her. She knew this should have been the least of her worries, but she couldn't help the way she felt. She was equally bothered by Blake's new willingness to miss a day from work. Like her, he'd never liked being absent, but it was now pretty obvious that he had no problem doing whatever he had to in order to spend time with that tramp. Kennedi knew this because he worked all the way in downtown Chicago at an ad agency, and there was no way he could simply be taking his normal lunch break out here in Covington Park.

"I wonder if she's one of his coworkers," Patrice continued.

"No offense, P, but it really doesn't matter who she is, because the bottom line is that she's been sleeping with my husband all this time like she had every right to. The bottom line is that regardless of who she is, my marriage is over and my whole life is about to change forever."

Patrice slowed toward a stoplight. "I guess you're right."

They drove the rest of the way to the law firm without words, and soon they were stepping off the elevator at the office.

"It's to the left," Kennedi said, and they walked in that direction. When they arrived at Attorney Newman's suite, Kennedi turned the doorknob and went in. Patrice walked in behind her but went ahead and took a seat.

"Hi. I'm a little early, but I have an appointment with Attorney Newman."

"Your name, please?"

"Kennedi Mason."

"I'll let his assistant know you're here."

"Thanks."

The receptionist adjusted her headset, dialed the number,

and told the assistant that Attorney Newman's 2:15 appointment was there.

"She'll be right out to get you."

"Thanks again," Kennedi said, and sat down next to Patrice, who was reading a magazine she must have gotten from the rack across the room. But only minutes later, a petite and very attractive twentysomething young woman came out to get them.

"Mrs. Mason?" she verified.

"Yes."

"Please come this way."

They followed the woman down a long corridor and into a medium-size conference room.

"Attorney Newman will be in very shortly, but can I get either of you something to drink? Coffee, tea, bottled water, soda?"

"Actually, I'll take some water," Patrice said.

Kennedi took a seat. "No, thank you, I'm good."

The assistant left the room and Patrice elbowed Kennedi. "The least you could do is hydrate your body."

"I will. Just not now."

"Kennedi, I don't want to keep harassing you, but if you don't take better care of yourself, you're going to get sick."

"I'll be fine."

"No, you won't be. If you don't eat, you don't drink, and, according to you, you're not even getting proper sleep, then how do you expect to survive? How do you expect to deal with everything you're going through?"

"You worry too much."

"Well, you don't worry enough. At least not about yourself."

"I'll get something later when I'm back at home."

"I wish you wouldn't be so difficult."

Kennedi smiled. "I love you, too." Patrice smiled back at her, and then the door opened.

"Kennedi," Attorney Newman said, shaking her hand. "It's good seeing you."

"It's good seeing you as well. This is my best friend, Patrice Johnson."

"Nice to meet you."

"Nice meeting you, too."

"Sooooo. What brings you in today? When you called this morning, you said it was sort of an emergency situation, so I'm glad I was out here in the suburbs and not at the downtown office. Oh, and by the way, the accountant I asked to join us works a couple of floors up and is on his way down here right now. Although you probably should go ahead and tell me what you'll be needing him for so I can be sure I've chosen the right person."

"I have the winning numbers for this week's Mega Millions game. All of them, including the Mega Ball."

"Whoa," he chuckled. "Yes, that would definitely constitute an emergency situation. Unbelievable."

"I know. I've known since yesterday and it still seems unreal."

Attorney Newman relaxed farther into his chair and laughed. "Wow."

"That was my reaction, too," Patrice said, laughing with him.

Kennedi was still upset about her run-in with Blake but still managed a smile.

"Well, congratulations. Also, I have to say that I'm now very glad I chose the accountant that I did, because he's one of the most competent professionals we deal with. He specializes in taxation, and he knows some of the best money managers in the business. As a matter of fact, two of those managers are part of the reason he's so independently wealthy himself."

"Thank you for contacting him."

"No problem at all. I was glad to do it, but even more so now that you've told me about all the money you're about to come into. You hear so many stories about people who win or inherit millions of dollars and how they never even take the time to plan out everything. They act hastily and irresponsibly, and the next thing you know, they're broke."

"Very true," Patrice said. "And I think the reason this happens to certain people is because they've never acted responsibly with any amount of money. And if you can't do the right thing with twenty thousand dollars, you certainly won't be able to handle seven or eight figures."

"Exactly," Attorney Newman agreed.

Just then, his assistant knocked at the door and walked in, escorting a man who must have been the accountant.

"Thanks, Karen," Attorney Newman said as she left. "Miles, thanks for coming. Kennedi Mason, this is Miles Avant. Miles, this is Kennedi Mason and her friend Patrice Johnson."

The three of them exchanged greetings and Miles took a seat. He was at least six foot two, dressed impeccably, and strangely enough, he was handsome—strangely because Kennedi expected a numbers expert to look just a bit more boring and a lot more studious, so she hoped he was as good as Attorney Newman had claimed.

"Well, Miles, I think you'd better brace yourself for what I'm about to say," Attorney Newman said.

"Okay."

"You know that mystery lottery winner they've been talking about on the news for the past couple of days?"

"Yes."

"Well, you're looking at her."

Miles sat up straighter. "Is that right?"

"Yes, and that's why she needs our services."

Miles switched his attention to Kennedi. "Congratulations."

"Thank you."

"I guess we've got our work cut out for us," Miles told them.

"That we do," Attorney Newman added. "I'll be handling her will, trust, and all of the estate planning, but we'll need you to do whatever it is you numbers people do with large sums of money like this."

"Of course, I'll do my absolute best."

What else was he going to say? That he was going to do his worst? Especially since Kennedi was sure he'd be charging a pretty hefty fee, the same as her attorney. But just as quickly as she'd had these sarcastic thoughts, she tried tossing them from her mind. She tried to rid herself of any skepticism because she knew this was all because of Blake. She knew this was all because of the way he'd deceived her and because she wasn't planning to trust another man for as long as she lived. She would have to deal with Attorney Newman and Miles Avant because she needed them, but after that she was through with any and every thing that resembled the male of the species.

"I think the first thing we should do is schedule at least two and possibly three more meetings before you claim your winnings," Miles began. "We have a lot to go over and a lot to get in order, but I'm thinking we can do this by early next week. Today is Thursday, so if we schedule the next meeting for tomorrow and another on Monday, you should be pretty set by Tuesday or Wednesday."

"Before we go any further, though," Attorney Newman said, "there is something I have to ask. I assume there's a reason why Blake isn't present, but it would help if you can tell me why. I hate having to get so personal, but we sort of have to know."

Attorney Newman had become acquainted with Blake when he and Kennedi had hired him to draw up their latest wills and power of attorney documents, so Kennedi had wondered when he would ask about him. "Long story short, we're getting a divorce."

"I see."

"Is that going to be a problem?"

"It could be. You see, if we were talking about a gift or some form of an inheritance, he wouldn't have any entitlement to it, but lottery winnings fall into the category of marital property, and that makes it a lot trickier."

"Well, I may as well tell you right now that I don't want him walking away with any of it," she said matter-of-factly. "Not under any circumstances."

"I understand."

"And I'll tell you why," Kennedi continued, her voice elevating. "He's the one who's been having an affair, he's the one who walked out on me, and he's the one who wants a divorce. So as far as I'm concerned, he barely deserves to live, let alone get any of my money." Patrice rested her hand on top of Kennedi's arm, and Kennedi tried to control herself. "I'm sorry."

"It's no problem at all, and I'm the one who's sorry that all of this is happening to you. Maybe we'll get lucky and Blake won't have the nerve to fight for anything."

"Maybe," Kennedi said, but knew it was wishful thinking.

"However, if he does try to go after some of the money, we'll come at him from every angle. Just the fact that he's already deserted you will give us at least some ammunition, and before it's over, I'll come up with a whole lot more."

"I appreciate anything you can do."

"That's what I'm here for."

"What would happen if she held on to the ticket until after the divorce is final?" Patrice wanted to know.

"I wish it were that easy, but my best advice would be that Kennedi should make her winnings known up front so that if we do end up in some sort of court battle, neither Blake, his legal counsel, nor the judge will be able to say she tried to conceal property that potentially belonged to both of them. It may not seem like it now, but in the end, it will be better to just deal with all of this head-on until everything is finalized."

Attorney Newman and Miles asked Kennedi a few more basic questions and then they prepared to adjourn.

"Oh, and before I forget," Attorney Newman added, "have you decided where you're going to keep the ticket between now and next week?"

"In a very safe place. It's not that I don't trust you or Miles," she lied, "but I think I'll feel a lot more comfortable if I keep the exact location to myself."

"I agree," he responded. "I just wanted to make sure it'll be secure for the time being."

"Well, if you want," Miles said, standing up, "you can follow me up to my office, and I'll have my secretary get you onto my calendar for tomorrow morning. I think I'm pretty free, but it won't hurt to check for sure."

Then Attorney Newman stood. "I'll try to sit in at the beginning and then we'll figure out what day you and I should get together for everything else we need to get drawn up."

Miles lifted his leather organizer from the table. "I'll also contact our number one investment guy so we can set up a meeting with him for Monday."

"Sounds good," Kennedi acknowledged, but she couldn't help thinking how overwhelming this was all going to be.

Deep down, she couldn't stop thinking about Blake, that woman, and how they deserved whatever they got. Even if she would have to be the one who gave it to them.

Chapter 5

Kennedi stared at the huge wedding portrait of her and Blake, the one that hung over the fireplace in the family room, and had a mind to snatch it down with all her might. As a matter of fact, she was now contemplating total destruction of every single thing that reminded her of that low-life she'd called her husband for the last ten years. She didn't want to hate him and was trying her best not to, but her efforts toward maintaining a forgiving heart, something she'd never had a problem with in the past, weren't working. Her mother had taught her a long time ago that God was a forgiving God and therefore expected everyone else to act in the same manner, but for the first time in a long time, she couldn't see herself doing it. Not after the way Blake had broken their marital vows. Not after the way he'd smiled in her face for months and months and all the while was bedding down with someone else.

But regardless of how outraged she was, there was still this underlying layer of sadness that she couldn't seem to rid herself of. Partly because she couldn't stop thinking about the day they'd met and how quickly they'd fallen in love with each other, and partly because the more she thought back, the more she regretted not paying attention to all the signs she'd talked about earlier with Patrice—signs she easily would have noticed had she not loved and trusted him so completely. Now she wondered if maybe she'd been more aware of what Blake was up to, she could have called him on it in time for them to seek out counseling. Maybe she could have stopped this whole disaster from ever happening.

Although what she wanted to know more than anything was where they'd both gone wrong. Where she'd gone wrong. Especially since they'd always seemed so happy with each other. In all honesty, Kennedi hadn't just *seemed* happy, she *was* happy. She was content and had always been very proud of how close they were as a couple. She'd always been extremely proud of the fact that they rarely argued and when they did, they never stayed angry for any extended periods of time. Not to mention she and Blake seemed to have so much in common that she couldn't imagine how he could have possibly entertained the idea of having an affair, let alone actually indulging in one. But this just went to show there were no guarantees about anything. There was no such thing as living happily ever after.

Kennedi finally sat down on the sofa but then quickly stood back up and headed into the kitchen. Once there, she pulled a wineglass from the cabinet and a bottle of Riesling from the refrigerator, opened the bottle, and filled the crystal goblet to the rim. They rarely kept alcohol of any kind in the house, but two months back, when she and Blake had invited over a couple of friends for a visit, Blake had decided to pick some up. Although as it had turned out, their company had taken a rain check and Blake and Kennedi had never gotten around to drinking the wine. Of course, she'd never drunk on a consistent basis anyway, but right now she needed something to help calm her nerves. She needed something to relax her body, and she was hoping this would help her sleep much better than she had the night before.

She took the bottle and glass back into the family room and dropped back down on the sofa. But just as she did, the doorbell rang. She wasn't sure who it could be, but what she did know was that she wasn't in the mood for any company. Not today, not tomorrow, not anytime in the near future.

But when it rang again, three times in a row, she went to the entryway.

"Who is it?"

"Uh, yes, I'm looking for Kennedi Arlene Mason."

"Okay."

"I have a delivery for her."

Kennedi frowned and then opened the door.

"Kennedi Arlene Mason?" he confirmed.

"Yes, that's me."

The man smiled apologetically. "You've been served."

Kennedi took the envelope from him and shut the door. Then she started back toward the family room, opened the envelope, and wanted to die. In her hand was a divorce petition, and all she could think was that Blake had to have filed this well before he'd told her he was leaving. How dare he do this to her. How dare he try dismissing her, fast and in a hurry, like she never mattered to him. Like they had not an iota of history together.

Kennedi tossed the petition onto the table, drank every drop of the wine she'd poured just before being interrupted, and then filled her glass to the top all over again. Then she leaned back on the sofa and pretended she didn't have a care in the world. Not about Blake or anything else.

After finishing off the entire bottle, Kennedi felt a little light-headed but couldn't stop thinking about that idiot she was married to. So she grabbed the phone and called him. And called him. And called him. But he didn't answer. She debated leaving a message but then hung up.

I don't love you anymore, I haven't for a long time, and I want a divorce. Kennedi replayed Blake's words over and over and over again, and then dialed his number in a heated fury one last time. Surprisingly, he answered.

"Hello?"

"You know what, Blake, you are, without a doubt, the most rotten and pathetic person I know."

"Kennedi, please. Why are you calling me?"

"Because I felt like it and because you owe me an explanation."

"Really? Well, that's strange, because I thought I explained everything pretty well when I saw you yesterday."

"Well, you didn't, and the very least you can do is talk to me."

"Why would I do that, when there's nothing else *to* talk about? Especially not after you acted like a complete fool at the restaurant earlier."

"Blake, what exactly did you expect me to do? Smile and then tell that tramp it was a pleasure to meet her?"

"This is crazy. And I have to go."

"Where are you?"

"Why?"

"Because I wanna know."

"Well, I don't think that's a good idea."

"Why are you doing this?"

"Because I've got a new life now, and you and I have said all we need to say to each other."

"Myyyy goodness. What has this woman done to you? Buried your nasty drawers somewhere out in her backyard? Has she got you so caught up that you no longer have a brain in your head?"

"I'm hanging up."

"No, just let me ask you one thing."

"What?"

"When did you file for a divorce?"

"Two weeks ago. But I asked my attorney not to have the papers served until today or sometime after because I wanted to talk to you first."

"So, the fact that I've loved you with all my heart and have been completely devoted to you since the beginning means absolutely nothing to you?"

"Kennedi, please, let's not do this."

"Just answer me."

"Why can't you just leave this alone?"

"Because after ten years, you owe me a legitimate reason for walking out on me."

"But that's just it, I've already told you what the deal is, and to be honest, I don't know how many other ways you want me to spell it out for you. I just don't love you anymore. Maybe the way people love their sisters, but not as my wife. End of story."

Kennedi's body went numb. It was true that yesterday he'd basically told her the same thing, but this time, she'd heard him loud and clear. She'd heard him in a way that couldn't be misunderstood, and she finally got it. So much so that her sadness and sarcasm quickly shifted to rage.

"You know what I hope? That you have a massive heart attack and die. Instantly. And preferably tonight, if you can manage it."

"See, this is why I didn't want to answer your call. But before I hang up, you should know that I had to work real hard to stop Serena from calling the police and pressing charges against you for that stunt you pulled today. So, if I were you, I'd consider myself warned."

"Warned? No, you're the one who'd better consider yourself warned, because if I see you and that tramp, *Serena,* as you say, out in public again before this divorce is final, both of you can expect a lot more than what happened today. More than both of your sorry little minds could ever imagine."

"Are you threatening us?"

"Take it whichever way you want to."

"Well, just know if you try anything, I'm having you arrested."

"Do I sound like I care about any of that? Do I sound like I'm worried about you, her, or the police? Do I?"

"You would if you knew what was good for you."

"And if you know what's good for you, you'd better pray to God I don't have HIV, because I'm sure you were too thoughtless and too stupid to even think about wearing a condom."

"Trust me. My girl doesn't have anything like that, so you don't have a thing to worry about."

"How do you know?"

"Because I know her better than that."

Kennedi laughed out loud. "I guess you really are that stupid."

"Look, I'm hanging up now, and I would really appreciate it if you would make this your last time bothering us."

"Blake, go straight to—" she screamed, but he hung up before she could finish. She had a mind to dial him back, but instead, she tossed the phone to the side of her and glared at their wedding photo again.

Then she picked up the empty wine bottle and flung it against the fireplace.

Chapter 6

If waking up with an excruciating headache was the real reward for drinking too much, Kennedi had no clue why anyone would ever choose to become intoxicated. She'd only drunk a full bottle of wine and felt miserable, so she couldn't imagine what the effect would have been had she consumed gin, vodka, or brandy, all of which had been three of her father's favorites until the day he'd died ten years ago. He'd struggled with a number of health problems, including high blood pressure, high cholesterol, and gout, but none of his ailments gave him reason enough to stop drinking on a regular basis. He wasn't per se an alcoholic, at least not by most people's standards, but he never went one day without having at least a couple of strong cocktails. But because of his frequent drinking habit and his refusal to drop the seventy-five pounds his doctor had practically begged him to get rid of, he'd ultimately had a massive heart attack and died.

Kennedi still remembered how devastated she and her mother had been and just how tragic it was to lose her father so instantly. This was also the reason she regretted wishing the same demise upon Blake yesterday evening. Lord knows she hadn't meant it, because no matter what he'd done to her, she certainly didn't want him dead. She would never hope for anyone's death, and the only reason she'd stooped to such a vengeful level, aside from her alcohol intake, was because of the way he was treating her—the way he was hurting her to the core and acting as if he had every right to do it. He was acting as if she should accept his affair with open arms and then congratulate him. Of course, that was never going to happen, but as of this very moment, she decided that her marriage truly was over for good and that it really was time for her to move on, the same as Blake kept advising her to. It was time Kennedi focused on Kennedi, and that was exactly what she was going to do. She'd be lying at an all-time high if she said she no longer loved her husband, but she knew she could never take him back, not after hearing him insist so adamantly that he didn't love her, and surely not after he'd put her life in danger.

Which reminded her, she'd either have to make an appointment with her primary care physician or go online to purchase one of those at-home kits one of her coworkers had told her about back when she'd learned her own husband was sleeping around, but regardless, Kennedi needed to take care of this right away. She needed to get herself tested so she'd have one less thing to worry about. Although who would have guessed that she'd ever have to worry about something of this magnitude at all? *She* clearly hadn't, and she could even remember how sorry she'd felt for her coworker when she'd confided in Kennedi about her own situation, and how the first thing Kennedi had thought was how glad she was that she'd never have to worry about being in a predicament where she would be too ashamed to go to her own doctor and then have to resort to some sort of Internet drugstore. This had been just a year ago, and little had she known Blake had already been placing her at risk.

Kennedi finally forced her body into an upright position and swung her legs over the side of the bed. Her head pounded more intensely than it had been while she'd been lying down, and she knew she had to take something. She'd been thinking that the aching would eventually subside without the help of any pain medication, but she could tell that wasn't going to happen. Getting drunk so hadn't been worth it, she thought, and then she closed her eyes and said, "God, please forgive me for doing this to myself. Forgive me for all of the hateful thoughts I've been having and for the violent nature I've been conveying. You know my heart is so much better than that, and I apologize. Then, Lord, I ask that you give me guidance and the strength that I'll need to make it through all that I am experiencing. In Jesus' name. Amen."

Kennedi couldn't remember the last time she'd prayed in the middle of the day, out loud and without warning, but she was glad she had. She was glad to know that she always had Him to depend on, even when she fell short and wasn't being the best person she could be.

After taking a couple of Extra-Strength Tylenols, Kennedi called her boss to let him know she wouldn't be in again today and that she was going to try her best to make it back on Monday. She could tell from the sound of his voice that he wanted to ask her what was going on, but he didn't. He sort of sat there for a couple of seconds, not saying anything, so Kennedi told him that she was sorry for her absence and that she would explain everything to him early next week. He seemed okay, but Kennedi didn't like having to be so secretive, not about her broken marriage or the large sum of money she was about to collect.

Next, she logged on to the Internet, Googled online drugstores, and placed an order as planned. Then she took a shower and got dressed for her appointment with Miles. Thankfully, her headache was much better, and strangely enough, she was starting to feel a little hungry. It had now been two full days since the last time she'd eaten anything, so she was glad her appetite had returned.

When she grabbed her handbag from the dresser, the phone rang and she went over to the nightstand to answer it. "Hey, Patrice."

"Hey yourself. And how are you this morning?"

"You mean aside from having to order an HIV test?"

"I hate that all of this is happening. But you're definitely doing the right thing."

"I know. Of course, I'm praying hard that it'll come back negative, but it's just the idea of having to do it. Other than that, though, I do feel somewhat better."

"I'm glad. I thought about you all night and I almost called you, but I had hoped you were resting."

"I was. But not until I finished off a whole bottle of wine and then had it out with Blake on the phone."

"Oh no. Did he call harassing you?"

"No. I called him."

"And did you say you drank a whole bottle of wine?"

Kennedi smiled because she could practically see the traumatized look on Patrice's face. "Guilty as charged."

"Wow. I knew you were upset, but not enough to start drinking."

"Well, believe me, I'm paying for it now, and it's definitely the first and the last time I'll be getting tipsy and having any hangovers."

"Still, what I wouldn't have given to witness you, of all people, getting your drink on. I'll bet that was a hilarious sight to see."

They both laughed and Kennedi said, "I don't know about that, but I do know it gave me the courage to say some very nasty things to Blake, some of which I now regret."

"Please. Serves him right."

"Oh, and before I forget, her name is Serena."

"That woman he was with yesterday?"

"Yep."

"And what exactly did Blake have to say for himself?"

"A lot. But what sank in the most was when he said he didn't love me. He said it with so much conviction this time, and I knew he meant it."

"I'm really sorry, girl."

"I appreciate that, but the bottom line is that Blake and I are finished, and I have to do whatever I need to in order to get over him."

"And you will. I know it'll take time, but you'll be fine."

Kennedi heard the call waiting tone. "Hey, hold on a minute."

"Okay."

"Hello?"

"Kennedi? Baby?"

"Yes. How are you?" she said to her mother-in-law.

"No, the question is, how are you? Blake just told me about the separation and, honey, I'm just sick over it."

"It's really unfortunate, but Blake has someone else now."

"He didn't tell me that. All he said was that it wasn't working out between the two of you and that he decided to move out."

"I'm sure he didn't want you to know that part of it."

"Well, I'm sorry, and I hope you know that your father-in-law and I are here for you if you need us."

"I know that, and thank you."

"Well, I won't hold you, but you take care of yourself."

"I will, and you, too."

Kennedi hit the flash button. "Okay, I'm back. That was my mother-in-law."

"So I take it she knows."

"Yeah, but Blake didn't tell her there was another woman involved."

"Figures."

"So, anyway, what's up with you? Because after taking up so much of yesterday with me, you must have a ton of work to do."

"Sort of, but if you need me to come with you to your meeting this morning I will."

"No, not at all. There's no reason for you to get further behind, and I can always call you if I need to."

"Okay, but it's really not a problem for me to delay a few things if I have to."

"Patrice, will you stop worrying?"

"I can't help it. I'm trying to stay strong for your sake, but deep down, my heart is really hurting for you. Last night, I even thought about Neil and how I would feel if I suddenly found out he was cheating. We've only been engaged for a few months, but after this thing with Blake, I can't help wondering if Neil has truly been the faithful man he's claimed to be the whole year we've been dating."

"Of course he has. P, please don't let Blake's infidelity cause you to question someone who I believe really loves you. Neil is a wonderful person, and from the time you met him, he's never given you a reason to think otherwise."

"I know that, but before Wednesday, you felt the same way about Blake and so did I. I tell you, Kennedi, I just can't get over it. I can't get over the way he's been sneaking around all this time and getting away with it, and now I don't put anything past anyone. Not even Neil. I love him, but starting today, my eyes and ears are wide open."

"I hate that this has affected you so negatively, because if Neil is being on the up-and-up with you the way I believe he is, then he doesn't deserve to have you doubting him."

"Maybe not, but I can't help the way I feel."

"Well, I just hope you don't start questioning him unnecessarily and feeling some great need to check up on him all the time, because it won't help your relationship in the least. I now realize that I obviously didn't check up on Blake enough and was way too lax with our marriage overall, but still, Neil doesn't deserve to be treated like he's some criminal suspect."

"I'm not saying I'm going to smother him or hire a private

investigator, although that might be a good idea." She laughed. "But what I am saying is that if he starts doing all this working-late stuff, traveling out of town on business too much, et cetera, et cetera, et cetera, then I'm going to be aware of it."

"I hear you, but just don't take it too far unless you have a reason. That's all I'm saying. And if anything, always make sure your lines of communication are open. Even when there are minor problems and petty disagreements."

"You're not thinking that's why Blake strayed, are you?"

"Maybe."

"Yeah, but even if you did have disagreements, I still don't see how that justifies Blake committing adultery. Maybe it's because I'm on the outside looking in and because I've never been married before, but right now I don't think there's any excuse anyone can come up with that I'd be able to condone. As far as I'm concerned, when people choose to get married they should honor their vows, and that's that."

"I agree, and I even have to say that I don't believe I ever would have had an affair on Blake, but at the same time, not every person is the same."

"Well, that's fine, but I just hope you're not blaming yourself for Blake's mistake."

"I'm not blaming myself, but I'll always wonder if things might have turned out differently if maybe we'd talked more."

"Hey, my business phone is ringing, so I have to run, but call me later, okay?"

"I will," Kennedi said. "Talk to you later."

She'd heard every point that Patrice had tried making, but she still couldn't stop thinking along the lines of could've, should've, would've—meaning what she could have done, should have done, or would have done differently if she had it all to do over again. But that was neither here nor there, and what she had to do now was switch her focus back to the present, focus on the impending matters at hand. She had to focus on what was sure to be one of the most talked-about divorces in Illinois history.

Chapter 7

I think the first thing we need to do is determine how much of the winnings you want to invest," Miles suggested to Kennedi, who was sitting adjacent to him at a table in a conference room similar to the one in Attorney Newman's office.

"I've been thinking about that on and off, and at the very least, I'd like to save around fifty percent of the total amount I receive after taxes."

"That's very smart and I'm glad to hear you say that."

"Actually, I was thinking more along the lines of sixty percent, but I guess that sort of depends on what the final number will be, since you always get quite a bit less when you take one lump-sum payment versus spreading the total over twenty years."

"This is true, and I don't blame you for opting to collect everything up front, because you never know what the future might hold."

"Exactly. Either I could die before the twenty years are up, or for all we know the lottery commission might go bankrupt."

Miles chuckled. "Let's hope not, but you do make a good point."

Kennedi smiled.

"Well," he said, flipping through a couple of pages in his yellow legal pad, "this is just an estimate, and a very conservative one at that, but I'm guessing that since the total is around sixty-three million, you'll probably end up with no less than thirty million free and clear."

Kennedi leaned back in her seat, trying to digest what Miles had just told her. She'd known the number was going to be a huge one, but at this very moment, it just didn't seem real. "That much, huh?"

"I'll bet you never would have imagined something like this happening, not in your wildest dreams."

"No, I wouldn't have. Not ever. And especially since I don't normally play the lottery in the first place, my chances of winning should have been pretty much impossible."

"Stranger things have happened, though, and while winning the lottery is a rarity, people do win all year long. You see them on television and in the newspaper all the time."

"I know, but with the exception of my husband, I don't think anyone truly believes they'll really win. I know I never expected anything like this, anyway."

"Well, maybe not, but you are in fact going to be thirty million dollars richer than you were."

"Still, the whole idea of this is just crazy."

Miles laughed and so did Kennedi.

"But getting back to the planning part of this, since you

already know for sure that you're going to save and invest about fifteen million, you and I can focus on the other half."

"Were you able to make an appointment with the money manager you mentioned yesterday?" Kennedi asked.

"Yes, I spoke with her right after you left and we're all set to meet with her this afternoon around two, if that works for you."

"That's fine."

"I'd originally had someone else in mind, but the more I thought about it, the more I realized Penelope O'Connor would be the best person for the job."

"Actually, I've seen some of her advertisements. Her office is downtown, right?"

"Yes, so we'll have to leave about twelve thirty or one, so we'll have time to get down there and find parking. Penelope has worked with millions and millions of dollars and has a number of wealthy clients, so I think you'll be happy with her services. Plus, she's very discreet."

"Good."

Miles flipped through his pad of paper again. "Now for the other part of this. I'm aware of the situation with your husband, but do you have any children or parents that you'll be wanting to offer a gift to?"

"My parents are both deceased."

"I'm sorry to hear that."

"And we have no children."

"Any close relatives or friends?"

"Yes, my mom's two sisters, and they each have two children, and then you met my best friend, Patrice, yesterday."

"I assume you're planning to give something to each of them?"

"Yes."

"Have you thought about how much?"

"Somewhat, but I need to think about it a little more and will let you know by Monday."

"Okay. Then the next thing would be charities, religious organizations, things like that."

"Well, before I do anything, I'm going to pay a tenth to my church."

"Good for you. I'm a tithing person myself. Have been since my college years."

"Really?"

"Yeah, and it would never dawn on me to not do it."

"Some people will think I'm crazy for giving three million dollars to any organization, let alone a church, but I know it's the right thing to do. There was a time when I didn't believe in giving ten percent from every paycheck, but the more I grew in my faith, the more I realized God was the reason I was blessed enough to have my job in the first place, and I've never looked back. Plus, I learned very quickly that when you give from the heart, God repays you over and above that."

"Always. And not only do I pay my tithe to the church, but there are a number of elderly members at my church who can barely make ends meet on their fixed incomes, so a couple of years ago, I started paying their utilities for them. And another thing I do is give a monthly check to one of the homeless shelters about thirty minutes south of here and also one to an area orphanage."

"That's wonderful." Kennedi was definitely impressed. Especially since Blake had never been the most giving person she'd ever met. He did give at church, whenever he found time to attend, but he never went out of his way to help anyone less fortunate than he was. As a matter of fact, he sometimes seemed sort of put out whenever he had to buy gifts for his own parents on holidays.

"I just wish more people would do the same, because if they did, they'd realize how rewarding it is, and, of course, the world would be such a better place."

"It would be, and that's why I'm going to set up a meeting with my pastor and the finance committee so that I can make sure every dollar will go toward helping people. I realize the church has operating expenses, but there are so many people who are in need, and I don't want to ignore that."

"That's a good idea."

"Another organization I want to donate to is the Susan G. Komen Breast Cancer Foundation, because my mother died from breast cancer."

"Do you know how much?"

"Maybe about a hundred thousand and possibly a little more."

"Okay. Anything else?"

"Well, actually, yes, but first can I ask you a question?"

"Sure. Go ahead."

"Attorney Newman mentioned that you were pretty wealthy, and if that's true, then why are you still working as an accountant?"

Miles chuckled. "I get that all the time. But to answer your question, I do it because I honestly love my job. I don't take on nearly as many clients as I used to and mainly only handle special cases like yours, but I can't imagine not working with numbers. Not to mention I also find great joy in volunteering my services to lower-income people during tax time."

"That's very kind of you, and so uncommon."

"Now, I will admit, though, that there are certain months that I do take off completely, but again, I really enjoy what I do, and it will be a long time before I consider retiring," he went on, but was interrupted by a knock at the door. "Yes."

"How's everything going?" Attorney Newman said, walking in and taking a seat.

"Great," Miles answered.

"Right now we're talking about gifts."

"Good. Well, I just wanted to stop up for a few minutes, but I can't stay long because one of my clients called for an impromptu appointment. But what I was thinking was that maybe you and I could meet later today or first thing on Monday."

"Monday would probably be better, because Miles and I are meeting with a money manager this afternoon."

"Of course. Monday will work fine. So, who did you go with?" Attorney Newman asked Miles.

"Penelope."

"Oh, then Kennedi, you'll be in great hands."

"That's what I hear."

"She's amazing. And personable, too."

"That really helps," Kennedi added. "Also, I do have some news."

"Which is?"

"After I got home yesterday evening, I was served with divorce papers."

"Is that right?"

"Yeah."

"Well, I guess he didn't waste any time, and actually this might work in our favor, because not only has he deserted you, but now he's made it known that he wants out of the marriage for good."

"So is there anything I need to do?"

"No, not this weekend, but you and I will talk in more detail on Monday."

"Sounds fine."

Attorney Newman stood up. "Okay, then. And I'll let the two of you get back to what you were doing before I interrupted you."

"Thanks so much for stopping by," Kennedi said, happy to know that she had someone like Attorney Newman in her corner.

"No problem. I'm glad to do whatever I can for you."

"Thanks again."

After Attorney Newman had left, Kennedi and Miles talked for another hour and then headed downtown to meet with Penelope. Miles had offered Kennedi a ride with him, but she'd told him that she had some errands to run right after the meeting and that it was probably best that they drove separately, which was true. However, it was more because she'd thought riding in the car with him was just a bit too personal. She did feel comfortable with Miles from a business standpoint, more comfortable than she'd expected, but riding in the same car all the way down to the Loop was something different, and she was glad he'd understood.

Now, though, she was on the way back to her suburb and had just turned her radio to one of Chicago's top R&B stations, but a hair product commercial was airing. Kennedi considered switching to another station, but since she always enjoyed this one, she left it where it was. Plus, traffic on I-94 East was already piling up, so she knew she might as well be patient, anyway. Which was fine, because after meeting with Penelope, she definitely had a lot to think about. Stocks and mutual funds for long-term investments; money markets for easy access, general spending, and so much more. She wasn't completely in the dark about these matters, not after working in human resources and having to deal with employee 401(k) accounts, but she'd still heard and learned more today than ever before and was glad. Penelope had explained everything in a very organized manner, and Kennedi could see why she held such a praiseworthy reputation. To put it plainly, she knew her job well, and she couldn't thank Miles enough for connecting them.

Kennedi continued down the expressway in what seemed like slow motion; she rested her elbow inside the window and then her head inside the palm of her hand. All of this creeping along was starting to wear on her, but thankfully, she only had a few more miles to go.

"Man, did you hear this morning that the person who won the Mega Millions still hasn't come forward yet?" the lead radio personality announced.

"Yeah, man, I heard," radio personality number two acknowledged. "What they're probably doing is gettin' all their ducks in a row so they'll be ready to flee the country at a moment's notice. Because you know every fifth cousin, so-called cousin, friend from kindergarten, and everybody else will be trying to get their hands on some of that dough."

"You can say that again. Those fools'll be swooping down

like mammoth vultures." Personality number one poked fun, and they both cracked up.

"They'll be hearing from relatives they haven't heard from in twenty years, the kind that will have an attitude if they don't get anything."

"Attitude? Man, please. They'll be ready to kick some booty and take names later. They'll be acting like *they're* the ones who won the doggone money."

They both laughed again.

"Shoot, I hear you, because with the exception of Jesus, you can't put anything past anyone when it comes to money. Money makes people insane."

"That it does. But you know who I really feel sorry for, though?"

"Who?"

"Whoever this person works for. Because you can bet they won't be getting any two-weeks' notice."

"You can say that again. Their employee is outta there. And actually, if the winner is a woman and she's listening, I want to be the first to say, baby, I'm available. I mean, I'm married, but that's only a minor detail," male personality number two joked.

Kennedi couldn't help laughing herself and then tried to call Patrice to tell her what she'd just been listening to, but she got her voice mail instead. She'd already called during her drive downtown to let her know how the meeting with Miles had gone, but she wanted to let her know about the meeting with Penelope as well.

"Hey, P, I'm in traffic and just thought I'd check in. I should be home in about twenty minutes, though, so give me a call."

Kennedi looked through her rearview and side mirrors and

then changed lanes. Traffic still hadn't picked up, but finally, she only had a few exits to go. So she switched to a different radio station and without warning thought about Blake. She'd thought about him earlier, a few times to be exact, but she'd pushed him out of her mind on each occasion. But now she couldn't stop herself from thinking about him and how she'd be so much happier about winning the money if they still had a marriage. He'd always talked about winning millions and what they would do with it. He'd talked about all the traveling they would do, the type of house they would build, the second home they would purchase somewhere south and near the ocean, and how they would never have to worry about money or bills for the rest of their lives. It was true that they'd never lived in poverty and had always been very responsible with the money they earned from their respective jobs, but Blake had always longed for just a little more than ordinary. Just a little more than average. But today, that was a trivial point, because the reality was that Blake had delightedly and voluntarily moved out and was acting as though their divorce was already final.

Kennedi turned in to her subdivision and was relieved to be home. That is, until she saw Blake's SUV backed into the garage and then frowned. He'd said he'd be back this weekend to get the rest of his things, but she'd thought for sure he'd meant Saturday or Sunday, because he normally worked on Fridays. But instead, here he was unannounced, and now she had to prepare herself to see him. Deal with him was more like it.

After leaving her car, Kennedi went inside and tried her best to hang around downstairs. She could hear him walking across their bedroom, and while she'd decided this morning that she wouldn't think bad things or act in a violent way, she could already feel her blood rushing through her veins. The reason: she just couldn't tolerate Blake coming into their house, gathering up his belongings, and then taking them to the home of his mistress. He hadn't confirmed where he was now residing, but Kennedi knew that's where he was staying.

She went through the mail that Blake obviously had had the audacity to bring in, and then she went into the family room and sat down with a magazine. But after reading only a couple of sentences here and there, she went up the stairway. As expected, she found Blake pulling from his closet one piece of clothing after another. He even looked at her for a split second but then turned his attention back to what he was doing and basically ignored her.

"Oh, so I guess you don't have anything to say?"

"Kennedi, please don't start with me. I came to get my things, and I was hoping to do it peacefully."

"You've moved in with her, haven't you?"

"What difference would it make if I have?"

"A lot, because you're still married to me."

"Not for long."

Kennedi bit her lip. She didn't want whatever this was they were having to turn into a screaming match, but it was all she could do not to respond.

"I'm really trying my best to be civil about this," Kennedi finally offered.

"After the way you clowned yesterday afternoon and then again last night on the phone, I rather doubt it."

"Well, maybe if you explained this to me, I wouldn't have to get so upset. I mean, believe me, I do get the fact that you don't love me and that we are never going to be together again, but there's a part of me that needs to know how this happened. Why it happened."

"I don't know exactly how. It just did. And if it'll make you feel better, it wasn't that you did anything in particular. I just think people eventually outgrow each other, and to be honest, I wanted out of the marriage long before I started seeing Serena."

"Then if that's true, why didn't you say anything?"

"Because I was hoping that I would eventually feel better about us. Except I never did."

"But I guess you feel just peachy about this Serena chick."

"You know, Kennedi, I don't want to hurt you any more than I already have, but I must say, life is too short to be miserable, and I've never been happier with anyone than I am with Serena. And I'd be lying if I said I was sorry for finding the woman of my dreams. She's my true soul mate, and maybe one day you'll be able to find the same thing."

Kennedi glared at him and didn't know what to say. Not after feeling the knife he'd just gouged straight through her heart.

But he continued. "You know, actually, I need to apologize to you, because the more I've thought back on our relationship, I don't think I ever really loved you the way a husband should love his wife. I mean, I did love you, but I was never head-over-heels *in* love with you," he said, grabbing another group of clothing and acting as though he'd just told her how nice the weather was outside.

Then he went down the stairs and out to his vehicle, and that's when Kennedi lost it. That's when she stormed into his closet and took as many pieces of clothing as she could handle from the rack and tossed them down the stairway.

She went back and forth grabbing everything she could get her hands on and tossed each and every garment until a huge pile had accumulated. But then Blake came back inside the house and caught her.

"What are you doing?" he yelled. "And why?"

"Because I felt like it. That's how we do things, remember? You felt like moving out, and I felt like helping you."

"You're sick."

"No, I'm perfectly fine, and all I want is to get you and your crap out of my house."

"In case you've somehow forgotten, this is my house, too," he informed her while picking up some of his belongings from the floor and carrying them outside, making multiple trips.

Then he came back up the stairs again and said, "This house is both of ours, so you might as well get good and ready to place it on the market. Either that or you can buy me out."

Kennedi folded her arms and laughed like she was at a comedy show. "You think I plan on staying here? Pleeease!"

"Actually, I do, because no matter how much you're trying to talk all big and bad, you know you don't have anywhere else to go."

"Hmmph."

"Hmmph is right," he mimicked, and it took every ounce of discipline in Kennedi not to tell him about the money and how she no longer needed this house or anything else they'd acquired together. She wanted to tell him that if he wanted to, he and that tramp of his could move in the very moment she moved out. But instead, she continued snickering at him, all while he made two more trips between the bedroom and the garage. Then Kennedi sat on the chaise and watched him go through his dresser drawers, pulling out underwear and miscellaneous items. Which was fine until he opened his mouth again.

"You know, with the way you're acting now, I no longer feel the slightest bit guilty about my affair, and if you want to know the truth, I feel more free and relieved than ever. You've made this so much easier for me than it would have been," he proclaimed, and then went back downstairs.

This, of course, sent Kennedi into a rage, and she was glad he hadn't taken all of his suits out of the closet yet, specifically his two most expensive getups by Armani, those he'd saved up for for months, so he could purchase one last year and another only a month ago.

Kennedi pulled them both from the rack, laid them across the bed, rushed over to her nightstand, and snatched out a pair of scissors. Snip, snip, snip. Snip, snip, snip. Snip, snip, snip. Snip, snip, snip.

"What in the world are you doing?" Blake bellowed out, and pushed her away from what now looked like two blazers designed with three-quarter sleeves and pants that looked more like knickers.

"So, tell me," she said coldly, "are you *still* feeling more free and relieved than ever?"

"I oughtta slap the taste out of your mouth," he threatened, and moved toward her.

"I hope you do," she spat back. "I wish you *would* put your hands on me, because, brother, you'd be doing me more favors than you realize."

She waited for a reaction, but all he did was walk away. Kennedi even followed behind him, yelling every word she knew she would have to pray about, but he still didn't respond. What he did do was go back outside, get into his SUV, and take off.

Kennedi watched until he was out of sight. While she'd already accepted the fact that their marriage was over, after this, she knew they were nothing more than common enemies. She knew they would never be friendly with each other again.

Chapter 8

It was Sunday morning, bright and early, and Kennedi lay in bed debating whether she should attend church or not. As it was, she hadn't made it to services last week, but with the way she was feeling at the moment, she was thinking it might be best for her to simply remain in bed. But on the other hand, maybe attending morning worship and hearing a good sermon might make her feel better. Maybe getting out of the house was the nice little pump-up she needed and the one thing that would help keep her mind occupied. Because so far, since she'd opened her eyes, all she'd thought about was Blake and the confrontation they'd had on Friday. Kennedi still couldn't believe how angry she'd gotten, how she'd cut up two of his most prized possessions, and how she'd said some of the worst things she'd ever said to anyone. But at the time, she hadn't been able to control herself, and she'd tried her best to hurt him deep within his soul. She'd tried her best to inflict the same kind of emotional pain he'd burdened her with, although now she knew none of what she'd said or done had made any difference, because in the end, Blake had still left and never looked back. He'd driven away in his glory, and like it or not, Kennedi was on her own.

In the bathroom, she stared in the mirror and saw that she looked like some madwoman. Her hair was all over the place and she hadn't even bothered to cleanse and moisturize her face—not Friday night, not yesterday morning, and not last night again. She'd lounged around all day Saturday, and the most she'd done was order a pizza from one of the nearby Italian restaurants. Come to think of it, the delivery guy had looked at her rather strangely, right after she'd paid him, and now she knew it was probably because of how *interesting* she'd been looking. He'd probably thought she wasn't quite right in the head or that she simply didn't care about the way she looked. Neither of which was true, but she couldn't deny that she'd sort of been wallowing in her sorrow. She'd told herself more than once that she was okay with losing Blake and perfectly fine with being single, but there was still a small part of her that would need a bit more time to get used to each scenario. There was something inside her that needed more time to reach a real level of acceptance.

Kennedi sat on the side of the bed again, preparing to flip on the television, but then the phone rang.

"Hey," she answered.

"How are you?" Patrice asked.

"Okay."

"Did you sleep well?"

"Better than the two previous nights."

"I'm glad."

"So, what's going on with you? And how was dinner?" Kennedi asked, remembering that Patrice and Neil had gone to a new Moroccan restaurant out in the north suburbs.

"It was great. The food was wonderful and so was the atmosphere. We really enjoyed ourselves."

"Good."

"So, are you getting ready for church?"

"No, and I don't think I'm going to either, because to be honest, I'm really not in the mood. I'm not in the mood for going anywhere."

"I understand how you must be feeling, but I think it would be great for you to get out and about."

"I don't think so. At first I was considering it, but—"

"Oh, come on, girl," Patrice interrupted. "Neil is heading to some golf tournament with his brother, so we can even get lunch right after."

"Maybe another time."

"Okay, look." Patrice sighed, sounding serious. "I let you sit around the house all day yesterday because I figured you needed some time alone, but this is where it ends."

"Meaning?"

"Meaning I'll be by to pick you up in about an hour and a half. Praise and worship begins at nine thirty, and you and I are both going to be there."

"But—"

"But nothing. Good-bye," she said, and hung up.

Kennedi pressed the off button and set the phone on the bed. She still didn't want to go, but she knew Patrice wasn't taking no for an answer and would never stop harassing her until she changed her mind. So she went back into the bathroom, took a shower, smoothed her hair back into a bun, applied her makeup, and got dressed.

Now she was sitting and waiting for Patrice to get there, and she had to admit that she felt pretty good. She was actually looking forward to hearing Pastor Abernathy preach the Word. Kennedi had always loved the way he taught straight from the Bible and so had her mother, and it was probably because he did it with so much ease. He spoke so genuinely, and it didn't hurt knowing that in all the years since they'd been members of his church, he'd never gotten caught up in scandals. No extramarital affairs, no outside offspring, no money scheming, no anything. Of course, Kennedi knew he wasn't perfect and that he was just as human as the next person, but overall, he was undoubtedly a decent man. He was a great leader, and his wife had to have been one of the sweetest women Kennedi knew. Pastor and Sister Abernathy were two of the best Christian role models anyone could ask for, and Kennedi let them know it on a regular basis. She'd told them many times that she respected them no differently than if they'd been her own parents.

However, Blake's feelings toward the Abernathys and the church as a whole were something totally different. Kennedi had never been sure why, but for some reason, he'd never been all that cordial with the pastor or first lady. They'd constantly gone out of their way to greet him and make him feel welcome, but for the most part, he'd responded on the cool side. Of course, the only reason he'd even joined Abundant Life Missionary Baptist Church was that before he'd met Kennedi, he'd rarely gone to any church at all. He'd stressed more than once how he hadn't seen a real reason to, but right after they'd gotten married, Kennedi had talked him into joining her congregation. But now, as she thought back, she realized he'd clearly done this against his will. He'd only done it because she'd wanted him to, and this was the reason he'd always dreaded going and only attended every now and then. When Kennedi was young, she'd heard her grandmother talking about couples who were unequally yoked, but little had she known, she and Blake fell into that same category. Kennedi believed in God and loved Him with all her heart, but Blake pretty much could take Him or leave Him. Kennedi believed in the power of prayer, but Blake had never thought it made any difference. Kennedi believed marriage was until death do us part, but Blake obviously had a different philosophy on that subject, too.

It was amazing, the length of time it had taken her to see just how little she and Blake truly had in common, and had they not separated, she wasn't sure she ever would have paid much attention to it. She was positive she would have done what so many other married couples did daily, and that was forcibly convince themselves that they were made for each other—convince themselves that they just couldn't be happier with anyone else. Kennedi knew this wasn't the case for everyone and that there were plenty of husbands and wives who legitimately loved each other, but after this major falling out, breakup, or whatever you wanted to call it with Blake, well, she would forever have a hard time believing anything she couldn't see behind closed doors—twenty-four hours a day, three hundred sixty-five days per year. Even then, she'd want to be inside each individual's mind so she could witness firsthand what they were honestly thinking. It was a shame Blake had turned her optimism into such hardcore skepticism, but this was the reality. Sadly, this was the way she would view marriage and relationships from now on.

The choir sang in magnificent harmony and Kennedi slightly bobbed her head to the music. She hadn't wanted to be there, but now she was glad Patrice had convinced her to come. Praise and worship service had definitely lifted her spirits, and she felt better than she had all weekend.

When the choir finished their last selection, Pastor Abernathy stepped to the podium. As always, he was dressed in a classically elegant suit and looked most distinguished.

"Let's give our choir another round of applause," he began, and members of the congregation put their hands together.

"Isn't God a good God?" he continued.

"Amen" echoed from every direction, and there were at least two thousand people in the building.

"I tell you, there are so many times when I sit wondering how some people make it through life without Him. I wonder how they deal with trials and tribulations. I wonder how they manage to simply make it through yet another day."

"Isn't that the truth," one man acknowledged.

"You just feel sorry for them," added a woman sitting directly in front of Patrice, and Kennedi wanted to agree out loud with all that was being said, except she'd never been a vocal type of parishioner.

"Let's give God a great big hand-clap," Pastor Abernathy encouraged, and then waited for the congregation to settle down again. "Well, today is a very special day for all of us here at Abundant Life. You've seen him on national television, you've seen him featured in very reputable magazines, and I'm sure some of you have even read his books. I've known about him for years, but I only met this remarkable minister a few months ago at a leadership conference, and I liked him from the moment I met him. At the time, he was dealing with a lot of public scrutiny, but I'm happy to say that today, he's completely turned his life around and has the kind of testimony that every man and woman in this country should have an opportunity to hear. This great speaker and awesome man of God needs no real introduction, so without further ado, please welcome none other than *the* Pastor Curtis Black."

Kennedi, Patrice, and practically everyone else gave a standing ovation, and Pastor Black hugged Pastor Abernathy and patted him on his back. Kennedi hadn't heard a thing about his being there, so this must have been an impromptu visit.

Pastor Black smiled. "Thank you. Thank you so very much."

But the applause continued.

"Thank you. Thank you for offering such a warm welcome," he said, and the room eventually grew quieter. "This is the day the Lord hath made, so let us rejoice and be glad in it," he recited, and gazed out at the audience. "It truly is a wonderful blessing to be here sharing with all of you this morning, and I appreciate being given the opportunity. Pastor Abernathy told you that I was a great man of God, but the truth is, he's one of the greatest men of God I've met in a long time. He mentioned how he liked me from the beginning, but what I want each of you to know is that the feeling is beyond mutual. Right away, I could tell he had the utmost integrity and the highest level of moral standards I've ever known any minister to have. In just a very short period of time, Pastor Abernathy has become a true spiritual father to me, and no matter how much time passes, I know I'll never be able to repay him for all of the advice and wisdom he has blessed me with or for the way he kept in touch with me and prayed for my family when we were going through a very rough time."

Patrice nudged Kennedi and they looked at each other. Patrice seemed awestruck, and Kennedi knew exactly what she was thinking: that it should be a crime for any man to be this gorgeous. Especially a minister. Kennedi had seen him on television, just as Pastor Abernathy had stated, and had thought he was extremely handsome, but this in-person experience was ridiculous. The man could have signed multimillion-dollar modeling contracts anytime he wanted, and his voice was plain mesmerizing. Pastor Black spoke in a way that demanded one's undivided attention, and there was no way you could ignore him.

"Some of you may have seen my interview with Michael Price, and if so, you're well aware that the situation I found myself in wasn't a pretty one. The whole disaster was humiliating, not just for me, but particularly for my wife and family, and I will forever be indebted to all of them for standing by me and for still loving me just as much as always. As a matter of fact, Charlotte, baby, stand up. You, too, Matthew and Curtina." He motioned to his family, and his wife turned around and greeted everyone. Kennedi loved the fitted, royal-blue sheath dress she wore with a large-brimmed matching hat and could certainly see why Curtis had been attracted to her. Charlotte Black was stunning and looked every bit like the wife of a man with money, power, and high status.

Then there were the children. The son was a handsome little thing and the spitting image of his father, and the daughter was a cutie as well. She didn't look to be more than a year old, so Kennedi knew this must have been the child Pastor Black had had out of wedlock with his mistress. Kennedi thought it was interesting how his wife had picked up the little girl and was smiling—interesting because Kennedi didn't think she could accept a child her husband had conceived with another woman while still married to her. But then, who was she to judge anyone? How could she judge another living soul when her own marriage had basically blown up in her face? So, no, she would stop trying to evaluate Charlotte Black and her decision to reconcile with her husband, because if they'd been able to work things out, Kennedi was glad for them. She was happy they'd loved each other enough to do so and weren't headed to divorce court the way she and Blake were.

When the applauding ceased, Pastor Black continued. "I thank God for my family, and I'm very proud to have them here by my side. I say that because there was a time when I preferred visiting other churches alone because that way, I could do whatever I wanted without any questions. But that was the old me, and today I'm a noticeably changed man. I'm living proof that anyone can learn from his or her mistakes and that if you keep your faith in God, if you live your life the way He wants you to live it, everything will turn out fine. If you do right by other people, you'll be blessed in more ways than you can imagine. If you learn the act of forgiveness and genuinely execute it, you'll always be at peace. Forgiveness is good for the mind, body, and soul, and thank God, my wife and I finally, finally get that. We finally, after all these years, realized that holding grudges and trying to get revenge was the reason our lives were in such an uproar. We realized that if God forgives so willingly and unconditionally, then who are we to do anything different?"

Kennedi nodded in agreement, because she knew Pastor

Black had a valid point. It was the same point her mother had made over and over since as long as Kennedi could remember, but no matter how hard she tried, she wasn't anywhere near forgiving Blake. Maybe one day she would be, but regrettably, she didn't see it happening anytime soon. If ever.

"Oh my goodness," Patrice exclaimed, barely shutting her car door and snapping together her seat belt. "Can you believe how incredibly good that man looked?"

Kennedi shook her head. "You crack me up. But I do have to admit, girl, he's pretty much flawless."

"Shoot, at one point, I was checking him out so closely, I had to catch myself," Patrice laughed. "And then I started feeling so guilty, I could barely stand it."

"Why? Because Pastor Black is married and you're engaged to Neil? That wouldn't be it, would it?" Kennedi teased.

"Let's just say I'm really going to have to pray hard about the kind of thoughts I was having today. I mean, girl, they were downright lustful, and right in the middle of service, too. But on the other hand, it's not my fault that Pastor Black looks the way he does. That's *his* fault!"

Kennedi laughed more intensely. "You should be ashamed of yourself, Patrice Latrice Johnson."

"You *know* I hate that country name."

"I know you do. But that's still your name . . . Patrice *Latrice* Johnson. That's the name *Matilda Jane* Johnson gave you."

"Whatever."

Kennedi chuckled, because if there was one thing Patrice disliked, it was her birth name. Actually, she didn't see a problem with her first name or middle name individually, but it was the combination that irritated her. She'd said it sounded like some bad nursery rhyme. But when Patrice had asked her mother why she'd given it to her, all Matilda Jane would say was that she'd liked it and so had Patrice's father. Of course, Patrice had eventually stopped discussing it altogether and had decided that anyone with a name like Matilda Jane probably thought the name Patrice Latrice was a work of genius.

Patrice turned out of the church parking lot. "So, where are we eating today?"

"I guess that's your slick little way of changing the subject."

"I'm good, aren't I?" Patrice smiled and so did Kennedi.

"Actually, I'm fine with anywhere you choose."

"Well . . . what about the Moroccan restaurant Neil and I went to the other night? It really was awesome, so I definitely don't mind going again. Plus, I really want you to try it."

"Sounds good to me."

They drove along in silence for a minute or so and then Patrice said, "I was hoping I could wait until after we had lunch, but the more I keep thinking about it, the angrier I'm starting to get."

"What?"

"I wanted to tell you as soon as I picked you up, but I knew if I had, you would have been miserable the entire church service. Or ready to hurt someone."

"What?"

"That jerk Blake called me this morning."

"For what?"

"Talking some junk about how I'd better talk to you because if you destroy any more of his property the way you destroyed his suits, or if you come near him or that Serena chick again, not only will he have you arrested, but he's going to make sure you do time for it."

Kennedi turned her body completely toward Patrice. "You must be kidding."

"I couldn't believe it either, but I'll bet everything I own that he won't be calling me again. I checked him up, down, and inside out, and I made it very clear that he'd better never, not in his entire natural life, dial my number again."

"Gosh. Blake has a lot of nerve. I mean, did he forget that you and I are best friends?"

"Apparently he did, because he even tried to justify his affair to me by saying that he's human just like anyone else and that you shouldn't blame him or Serena for anything because they can't help how they feel about each other. Then, on top of all that, he said you should have the decency to understand when someone doesn't love you anymore."

"P, just stop. Don't say another word, because if I hear any more, I'll end up in jail, just like Blake keeps suggesting."

"I know how you feel, because he's got me wanting to do terrible things to him—and I'm not even married to that fool. But when it's all said and done, he's not worth it, Kennedi. He's not worth you getting into any trouble."

"I know that, but he's making it very hard for me to turn the other cheek, and the best thing he can do is stay away from me."

"I hear you."

"But hey, on a much more positive note, Pastor Black isn't the only noticeably handsome man we've seen this week, because that Miles guy looks pretty wonderful as well. I wanted to mention that to you the first day we met him, but with everything that was happening with Blake, I figured something like that was the last thing on your mind."

Kennedi heard every word Patrice was saying, but she didn't comment one way or the other, because her mind was set more on Blake and the fact that he kept threatening to have her arrested. His own wife. Not to mention that he was continually defending that whore he had betrayed her with and acting as though Kennedi was in the wrong.

But that was okay, because while Blake was so arrogantly riding high with his new love interest, Kennedi would still have the last laugh. She would laugh her little behind off and would do so as soon as this coming Tuesday. She couldn't wait to see the look on Blake's face the next time she saw him. Why? She knew it would be priceless.

Chapter 9

The big day had finally arrived, and Kennedi was somewhat overwhelmed by the media turnout. She had, of course, expected that every Chicago newspaper and television station would be represented, what with her residing in that particular area, but in the last hour, she'd also spotted cameramen and reporters from CNN, Fox News, and a slew of other national stations.

Now, after witnessing the whole press conference platform and seeing so many people squeezing into the room, she wasn't sure she was ready to be bombarded with tons of questions. Attorney Newman had told her that the news conference participation requirement tended to vary from state to state but that unfortunately, Illinois's lottery commission had made it necessary for all Mega Millions winners. She hadn't thought that was fair and wondered why issuing a general statement by press release wasn't enough, but she also couldn't deny that a part of her had wanted to take the more formal and publicized route as a way to get back at Blake. She'd wanted him to hear the news from everyone around him and then regret everything he'd done to her. She'd wanted him to realize what a mistake he'd made the day he'd rushed home from the gym and announced his plans to be with someone else.

"Your mom is so proud of you today." Aunt Lucy smiled, tears filling her eyes.

Kennedi hugged her tightly. She'd finally called both her mom's older sisters yesterday evening, told them the news, and then invited them to accompany her this morning. She'd sworn them to secrecy, and they'd pledged not to say a word to anyone, not even to their children. It had taken a bit of convincing in order to get them to believe this lottery news wasn't some joke, but now they seemed very excited about it. She did wonder, though, how they were going to feel once they learned about her separation from Blake, but oddly enough, they hadn't asked about him. She was sure they'd already started speculating, especially Aunt Rose, the nosiest person in the family, but thankfully, they still hadn't brought it up yet.

Aunt Rose reached over and embraced Kennedi, too. "Our sister would be the happiest woman on earth if she could see you right now."

"She does see her," Aunt Lucy proclaimed. "She's looking down on her at this very moment."

"I'm just glad both of you could be here with me. Both of you as well as Patrice."

"You know I wouldn't have missed this for anything," Patrice declared. "Not for anything I can think of."

They all chuckled and then Attorney Newman walked toward them. "Well, my dear, are you ready?"

"I guess so."

"You'll be fine," Miles promised, trying to set her mind at ease.

"Thanks for being here and for everything you've been doing to help me prepare for all of this."

"It's been a real pleasure, and I'll continue helping you in any way I can."

Kennedi locked eyes with Miles, and unlike the other times she'd met with him, she felt uneasy. Not in a negative way, but sort of like when you meet someone for the first time and realize you're attracted to them. Sort of like when you discover there's a certain level of chemistry between the two of you, yet you barely know one another.

But presently, that was the least of her worries, because Attorney Newman had just introduced himself as her representative, and right now, she was standing at the mahogany podium, adjusting the mic.

"Good morning."

"No," one of the female reporters disagreed, the one in a pure white pantsuit. "For you, this is a *fabulous* morning."

Everyone found humor in her comment and Kennedi grinned. "That it is. It's turned out to be the blessing of a lifetime."

"So, tell us," the woman in white continued. "What do you plan on doing with such a huge amount of money? We've heard that you're going to walk away with just over thirty million dollars, so do tell."

"Well, the very first thing I'm going to do is pay off every single creditor I owe, and then I'll be giving some of it to family members and friends. I'll also be giving money to my church and a number of other charitable organizations. My goal is to help as many people as I can and, of course, save enough to make sure I never have to worry about money ever again."

"Are any of the future gift recipients here today?" a gentleman in the back wanted to know.

Kennedi gestured to the side of her. "Yes. Three of them. Two of my aunts, as well as the woman I've been best friends with since elementary school. Fourth grade, to be exact."

"Did they know before today that you were planning to give them part of it?"

"No. But I'm sure they pretty much assumed I would be."

Everyone laughed and then another female reporter asked, "The other thing everyone throughout this country is probably wanting to know is how you did it."

"There was nothing systematic about it, so basically all I can say is that it just happened. Because the thing is, I've never been a regular lottery player, and I barely play more than a few times a year."

"That's amazing. And the winning numbers were randomly selected as a Quick Pick, is that right?"

"Yes. I never would have taken the time to write down anything specific, because to be honest, I never believed I would actually win."

"So, what prompted you to play last Tuesday?" a male reporter in a black suit inquired.

"I stopped by the convenience store near my home and heard another couple talking about how much they play the lottery and what they were going to do with the money when they won. They were raving about it so much, I figured since the jackpot was around fifty million dollars, I didn't have anything to lose. That was it."

A twentysomething young woman raised her hand. "I know this might be a bit on the personal side, but if you don't mind answering, I wondered if you have a boyfriend. And if so, how does he feel?"

"No, I don't have a boyfriend," Kennedi said, glancing at Attorney Newman, then quickly returning her attention to the media.

"She's right," Blake said loudly while entering the room. "She doesn't have a boyfriend. How could she, when she has a husband of ten years? How could she have a boyfriend when I'm standing right here before all of you?"

Kennedi was mortified. And how had Blake found out she was the winner? She knew the media would have certainly announced the date and time of the press conference, but as far as she'd known and per her request, her name still hadn't been disclosed. She refused to believe that any of the five people that did know—Attorney Newman, Miles, Patrice, Aunt Lucy, or Aunt Rose, the people she'd entrusted with such delicate information—would ever deceive her, and decided that maybe someone from the lottery commission had leaked her identity. Either way, she hadn't wanted Blake to find out until after the fact, yet now he was moving closer to the front, ready to take her head-on.

"Did you actually think you were going to get away with this? Did you actually think you could waltz in here, collect millions and millions of dollars, and pretend like I don't even exist?"

Kennedi watched every camera being repositioned toward Blake, and Attorney Newman stepped closer to the podium. "Mr. Mason, this really isn't the place for this, and if you'd like to speak to me when the press conference is over, I'd be happy to oblige you."

"For what? Because as far as I'm concerned, you don't have a thing to do with this. I'm sure you're probably representing my wife, but this is between her and me and only her and me."

Kennedi was at a loss for words and dreadfully humiliated. This was not at all the way she'd planned for this to turn out, and her strategy to get at Blake was backfiring.

Attorney Newman pulled the mic up higher, making it easier for him to speak into. "Ladies and gentlemen, it is with deep regret that we must now end this interview session, but please know that we thank you for your time and interest," he finished, and then rested his hand across Kennedi's back, directing her out of the room. Patrice, Kennedi's two aunts, and Miles followed closely behind, but Kennedi could hear the reporters firing one question at Blake after another. She could only imagine what he was going to tell them and wanted to stay there and listen. But when she paused, Attorney Newman lightly pushed her along and out the entrance.

In the parking lot, Attorney Newman said, "I was afraid this might happen, but not here. Do you know how he could have found out?"

Kennedi shook her head. "No. I have no idea."

"Well, it's probably just as well, because now that he knows, the sooner we'll be able to see what he's expecting. My guess will be one half of the entire amount, but we'll see what he comes to us with. In the meantime, though, I think it will be best if you decline all interview requests, because the last thing we want is for this to turn into some circus act. Blake's showing up here today has already gotten the media scrambling for more details, but I don't want you giving them anything from your side of the coin. We'll handle every aspect of this in court and nowhere else."

"Fine."

Attorney Newman pulled his BlackBerry from the inside of his suit jacket and checked to see who was calling him. "If you'll excuse me for a few minutes, I need to take this."

Kennedi nodded. "Please, go ahead."

"Actually, I need to check in with my office, but I'll be back as soon as I'm finished," Miles told her.

"Go do what you have to do. I'll be okay."

But as soon as Miles stepped barely ten feet away, Aunt Rose started in. "Kennedi, what's going on with you and Blake? I knew when we didn't see him here that something was wrong, but I didn't want to ask," Aunt Rose lied.

Kennedi sighed, because she wasn't in the mood to talk about any of this. "We're not together anymore."

"Since when?"

"Since last week."

"Why?" Aunt Lucy finally asked, but it was obvious she didn't feel comfortable prying, at least not as comfortable as Aunt Rose.

"Because he's been seeing someone else, and he wants a divorce."

"And he's already moved out of the house?" Aunt Rose interjected.

"Yes."

"And he's got the gumption to be tryin' to claim some of that money?" She frowned. "Shoot, if you ask me, the only thing you owe Blake is a nice tail-kickin'."

Aunt Lucy empathized with her niece. "Sweetheart, I'm really sorry that this has happened."

"It's life," Kennedi admitted. "And I'm not going to spend months and years dwelling on it."

"Good for you," Aunt Rose agreed. "Because that joker surely isn't worth it. Not if he was low enough to go out and lay up with some floozy."

"Rose," Aunt Lucy pleaded.

"I'm sorry, but where I come from, there's nothing worse than some lyin', cheatin' son of a gun who now feels like the wife he cheated on owes him something. That man has a lot of nerve, and as soon as he brings his little narrow behind out here, I'm telling him exactly what I think of him."

Aunt Lucy put her foot down. "Now, Rose, this is none of our business, so don't you even think about saying one thing to that man. This is something he and Kennedi have to work out."

Aunt Rose averted her eyes, clearly in disagreement, but didn't say anything. Kennedi could tell Patrice wanted to scream with laughter, and she was glad Aunt Lucy had cooled Aunt Rose down a notch.

"Here's that little sorry mackerel now," Aunt Rose mumbled under her breath when she saw Blake striding toward them.

But all he said to Kennedi in passing was, "You thought you were being clever, but I'll see you in court. I'll see you in court sooner than you think."

Kennedi watched him get inside his vehicle and wondered if he really had a chance at collecting fifteen million dollars from her. Half. One half of the entire check she would be receiving in four to six weeks.

The whole idea of it was enough to make her sick.

Literally.

Chapter 10

Well, if it isn't Miss Moneybags herself," Carson, Kennedi's supervisor, raved.

"I don't know about all that," she replied unpretentiously.

"Well, I do. You've got more money than everyone in this building put together, and there're easily five hundred people who work here."

Mary, Kennedi's administrative assistant, concurred. "Isn't that the truth."

"I guess I will be pretty comfortable," Kennedi admitted.

Carson grinned. "To say the least. And now I know why you took those days off last week. You had a lot to think about and a lot to get in order."

"I really did. And thank you so much for understanding."

"Actually, I'll understand even better as long as I'm included as one of those friends and family members you talked about during the press conference," Carson joked.

Kennedi and Mary laughed, and then five other human resources employees walked in. Roger, the benefits manager, reached his arms toward Kennedi and embraced her. "Congratulations, Mrs. Mason."

Kennedi cringed, because she'd never liked the way Roger approached any of the women in the company, including her. He had always been just a little too touchy-feely, and Kennedi, on many occasions, had thought he'd crossed the line and entered sexual harassment territory. But he was good about not crossing the line far enough for anyone to make any legitimate accusations. "Thank you."

"Well, I guess it goes without saying," Carson stated. "I'm about to lose my top HR specialist."

Kennedi smiled. "Unfortunately, yes."

"Two weeks?"

"Yes, and I'm sorry for giving such short notice."

"That's all the lead time we require, so you're not doing anything against policy. And to be honest, I'm not sure most people would stay around even that long."

"Kennedi," Greta, the mailroom supervisor, said, entering the area. "I heard the great news. But it's really too bad about you and your husband. I saw what happened during the press conference."

If Carson and the others hadn't been standing there, Kennedi would have told Greta exactly where she could go. Greta was the most negative person Kennedi knew, and the woman criticized every single coworker she came in contact with. Which was interesting, considering the fact that she was sorely unattractive, needed to have her teeth fixed, and clearly didn't have the best personal hygiene. Yet she always talked as if she was the best thing going.

Kennedi turned a half smile but didn't answer, and Carson intervened. "Why don't we go have a sit-down?"

"Sounds good."

Kennedi and Carson started toward Carson's office, but then Roger said, "If you need someone to help you choose the perfect floor plan for that new mansion that I know you're getting ready to build, I'm available."

"Really? Is your wife available, too? Because I think the three of us together could come up with some amazing ideas, don't you? Actually, the more I think about it, maybe I should just give her a call to let her know you offered both your services and then see if we can set up a time."

Mary snickered and walked away. Some of the others did the same. Roger stood there in silence, and Kennedi could tell he hadn't expected her to respond in the manner she had. To be honest, before learning about Blake's affair, she probably would have continued ignoring Roger's constant flirting, but not anymore. Not after painfully realizing that no woman deserved to be disrespected, in her face or behind her back.

In Carson's office, Kennedi took a seat.

"You won't believe this," he began. "But remember when I told you not too long ago that you were going to be my next manager for salaried employees?"

"Yeah."

"Well, Richard is moving to our facility in Madison, Wisconsin, and he's leaving at the end of this month. Which means I was just getting ready to promote you."

"What timing, huh?"

"Bad timing, to be exact, and I'm just sorry I hadn't been able to offer you the position before this week. You've always done over and above what's expected of you, and you were the perfect choice."

"Thank you for saying that."

"It's true. But I will admit that the most I would have been able to pay you would have been around fifty-five to start. I know that's a major increase compared to the forty thousand you're earning now, but it's still mere crumbs compared to what you just won."

"Still, I'm honored that you felt I was ready for management and that you were going to up my salary by nearly thirty percent. It means a whole lot, and I won't ever forget it. I won't ever forget how well you've treated me since I first started working for you or the way you encouraged me to learn everything I could."

"I knew you had a lot of potential, and that's why even though I had the other two specialists reporting to managers, I wanted you reporting directly to me. It was always my plan to groom you and steer you as far up the ladder as I could."

"You're a good man, Carson, and I'm really going to miss you."

"We'll all miss you, too, but I hope you won't be a stranger."

Kennedi swallowed a lump in her throat. "I'll certainly try not to."

As usual, Wal-Mart was busier than ever. It was well after six P.M., so the checkout lanes were filled with nine-to-fivers as well as people who probably had no schedule to keep at all.

Now Kennedi wished she'd either waited until later this evening to pick up the few household items she needed or possibly gotten up early enough to stop by Wal-Mart on her way to work in the morning.

But since she was already inside, she pushed her cart down the cleaning products aisle and stopped when she rolled in front of her favorite orange-scented, antibacterial dish detergent. It smelled heavenly, and it was one of the few things she made sure she didn't run out of. Blake had never understood why she chose to hand-wash their dishes when they had a dishwasher, but Kennedi had always enjoyed doing them this way since she was a child. She enjoyed dipping her hands in piping-hot suds, and she loved how spotless everything turned out when she was finished. She did use the dishwasher on occasion, but never more than once a week.

"Hey!" some lady screamed while stopping abruptly. "It's you! Hey, everybody, it's her. The woman who won all that money. Oh my God. I saw you on television yesterday."

Kennedi couldn't remember ever feeling so embarrassed, and she wondered if she would have to live like this from now on. She wondered if the idea of having any privacy would be no more.

"This is so exciting," the woman exclaimed. "Do you mind if I take your picture with my cell phone?"

Kennedi opened her mouth to say yes, she did mind, but before she could, at least six other people gathered around, and Ms. Photographer snapped the camera button immediately.

"How does it feel?" a gentleman with salt-and-pepper hair asked.

"I'll bet it feels wonderful," a younger gentleman added.

"Can I talk to you?" a young woman with two small children inquired.

Kennedi couldn't imagine why, but said, "About?"

"My boyfriend is in jail, and my landlord said that if I don't pay the rent by tomorrow, he gon' evict us. So if you can somehow find it in your heart to loan me fifteen hundred dollars, my children and I won't have to end up on the street."

Kennedi was flabbergasted, but for the sake of curiosity she asked, "You live here in Covington Park and your rent is fifteen hundred dollars?"

"No, it's seven fifty, but just in case Neeko don't get out of jail by next month, I'm gon' have to pay that rent, too."

Kennedi shook her head in disbelief and forced her cart through the crowd of customers.

"Oh, it's like that, huh?" the young woman spat. "You comin' into all that loot but now you got the big head and don't wanna help other folks out. But that's okay, and that's why I hope your husband take you for everything you got."

Kennedi left her cart at the end of the aisle and rushed out of Wal-Mart as fast as she could. She heard someone calling out to her, but she never looked back. She didn't stop until she reached her car and took cover.

What?" Kennedi declared when she drove into the driveway and spotted Blake's SUV. "This man must be out of his everlasting mind!" she complained, and then turned off the ignition and exited her Cadillac CTS. Then she stormed inside, ready for World War III.

Blake was leaning against the kitchen counter. "Why didn't you tell me?"

"Because I'm not obligated to tell you anything. You moved out, remember? And we're getting a divorce."

"But still, Kennedi, you could have told me."

Was he trying to sound like the reasonable and decent man she'd once believed him to be? Because right now, his tone was pleasant and didn't sound at all like the way it had over the last few days.

Blake sat down at the island. "I'm not here to argue with you. I just want to talk."

Kennedi dropped her leather tote on one of the chairs, her demeanor sarcastic. "Oh, so now you want to talk?"

"Yes. Is that too much to ask?"

"As a matter of fact, it is, because when I wanted to *talk*, you basically had nothing to say."

"You're right, and I'm sorry."

"Are you really, now? And why is that?"

"Because I was wrong. Wrong for showing up today and confronting you the way I did."

"Well, it's pretty much too late for apologies, Blake, because the damage has already been done. National damage, at that."

"I know, but if you'd just told me, none of this would have happened. I know you're upset and that maybe I didn't deserve to hear the news from you, but you still should have informed me."

"So who told you, anyway?"

"I have no idea. I received a message at work, but I couldn't make out the voice. I didn't recognize it."

"Was it a woman?"

"I think so, although as high-pitched as the person sounded, it could have been a man disguising his voice. Either way, someone thought I had the right to know about that press conference."

"What I want to know is why you're here. You moved out and filed for divorce, and if memory serves me correctly, you told me not to bother you again. Am I right?"

"That was only because you made me so angry, and sometimes we say things we don't mean when we're upset."

"Hmmph. You're too much."

"What do you mean?"

"Exactly what I said."

"Why are you being so cold?"

"Look, Blake, let's stop playing this ridiculous game of charades. I asked you a few minutes ago, and now I'm asking you again. Why are you here?"

"I know I've hurt you and that I'm probably the last person you want to reason with, but Kennedi, the situation is what it is."

"Meaning?"

"That I'm entitled to fifty percent of those lottery winnings. I checked, and Illinois law says that one half of that money is rightfully mine. It's marital property, and I just want to make sure you realize that."

Kennedi stood up. "Get out."

"I beg your pardon?"

"Get your sorry little behind up from that chair and get it out of here. Now."

"Have you forgotten that my name is on the title of this house just like yours is?"

"I don't care if Donald Trump's name is on it. I still want you out of here."

"Fine," he relented. "But when that check comes, I'll be expecting my part of it within twenty-four hours."

"In your dreams, maybe."

"Look, Kennedi, I've been trying my best to be civil, but don't make me sue you. Because if you force me to take this into court, I'm going after every red cent."

"If you don't get out, I'm calling the police."

"For what? To ask them to escort me away from my own property?"

Kennedi picked up the phone.

Blake slid his chair away from the island. "You're crazy, and while I thought you were pretty intelligent, I can see now that you don't have a clue when it comes to legal matters."

"You just don't plan on leaving, do you?" she said, pressing the on button and preparing to dial 911.

He headed toward the door leading to the garage and opened it. "Just so you know, I'm leaving because I'm finished saying what I need to say and not because you're instructing me to."

Kennedi fixed her eyes on him, and it was all she could do not to hurl the cordless phone against the back of his head.

"I'll be in touch," he announced as if they didn't have a problem in the world with each other, and then closed the door. He acted as though they hadn't just argued like two enemies and that there was no animosity between them whatsoever.

But Kennedi would make sure he knew differently. She'd make sure he knew she wasn't someone to be played with and that she would fight for months and years before she'd let that tramp Serena get her hands on one dime of that lottery money.

She would do whatever she had to, making sure Blake and his whore ended up with nothing.

Chapter 11

After arguing with Blake, ignoring a plethora of phone calls from the media, and then pricking her finger and squeezing blood onto a small sheet of paper, Kennedi was surprised at how well she'd been able to sleep. Eight and a half hours, to be precise. But she guessed it was because she'd finally gotten to a point where she was completely wiped out and her body had forcibly garnered the kind of rest it had needed. Now, though, she slipped on a pair of tan-colored pants and was preparing to head off to work. That is, until the phone rang and she glanced at the caller I.D. screen.

She shook her head but picked it up. "Hello?"

"Ms. Kennedi Mason?" a man on the other end inquired.

"Who's calling?"

"Is this she?"

"It depends on the nature of your call."

"I'll just take that as a yes," the man stated, and Kennedi couldn't believe the nerve of some of these people.

"My name is Jason Cruise with the Shaw-Winston Group, and I'd like to schedule some time to go over your investment plan."

"Actually, I've already taken care of that. I already have someone in place, but nonetheless, I do appreciate your call."

"Well, I'm not boasting, but I'm the best money manager in the Chicagoland area, so I really think it would be to your benefit if you gave me at least an hour of your time. Especially since I'm positive I could do a better job than the person you're working with currently."

"As I said before, I already have someone in place."

"Ms. Mason, with all due respect, I hear what you're saying, but trust me, if you stick with this other money manager, you'll be making a huge mistake."

"Why? Do you know her?"

"No, but if the person you've hired isn't me, then there's no way you could possibly receive the best advice available. I'm not trying to discourage you, but what I'm telling you is simply a fact."

It was obvious that this man wasn't taking no for an answer and wasn't about to give up on trying to change her mind. "Look . . . what did you say your name was?"

"Jason Cruise."

"Look, Mr. Cruise. For the last time, I've already made my decision in terms of who I want to manage my money, and if you must know, my accountant and my attorney believe she's the best person for me. So, if you'll excuse me, I have to get to work."

"Wait! That's all well and good, but the bottom line is that I'm the best man for the job, so will one o'clock or two o'clock this afternoon work for you?"

Kennedi hung up the phone. "My goodness," she uttered as if someone was listening. "These people are crazy."

As she started away from the nightstand, though, the phone rang again, and she saw that it was the same number and company as before. Jason Cruise was a real piece of work and clearly wasn't the kind of man who gave up very easily, but eventually, once he realized Kennedi would never answer his calls again, he would have no choice but to move on.

Over the next twenty minutes, the phone rang five more times, and while Kennedi refused to answer it, she did listen to each of the six voice messages that were left. Needless to say, one was from Mr. Cruise, now practically begging her to meet with him; one was from a guy employed with a totally different investment firm; the next two were attorneys from two different law firms, offering the best representation in town; and the others were just hang-ups. Kennedi deleted every single one of them and then dialed her phone company. She couldn't wait to have her number unlisted.

Kennedi said another prayer, dropped her HIV-test blood sample inside the FedEx drop-off box, headed onto the expressway, and flipped her radio to the same station she'd been listening to last week when the hosts had been discussing the undisclosed lottery winner. At the moment, the Morning Crew was chatting and cracking up about only God knew what, and Kennedi waited to see which celebrity they were razzing this time around. J Sampson, Melvin D, and Reba seemed to love Hollywood gossip more than anything else, and Kennedi couldn't deny her own interest and curiosity herself.

"See, what I'm thinking," Melvin D began, "is that as soon as this Kennedi woman found out she'd won the big jackpot, she gave the old boy the ax. Kicked brother-man straight to the curb and then called up her man on the side."

"You might be right," J Sampson agreed, and Kennedi audibly sucked in more air than normal. "Which is why I don't think she should be allowed to get away with this. This woman should have to pay up or else."

"If you ask me," Melvin D added, "she ought to be put in jail for trying to beat a brother out of his rightful cut of that money."

"Under the jail is more like it."

"That's cold," Reba finally commented.

"What?" J Sampson said.

"You guys are wrong for taking sides one way or the other, because how do you know the husband isn't the one who left and then found out his wife had won the money?"

"Exactly!" Kennedi yelled out, and changed lanes.

"Please!" Melvin D spurted out. "That's just like a woman to take up for another one, regardless of what the facts are."

"But that's just it," Reba argued. "We don't know what the truth is. And all the two of you are doing is sitting here speculating. You don't know any more than the rest of America."

"Maybe not, but I'll bet my next paycheck that she tried to dump him after the fact," Melvin D reiterated.

"Whatever," Reba said. "You and J can believe anything you want, but when the truth comes out, you'll both be tucking your tails."

"We'll see, and hopefully very soon," J Sampson proclaimed.

"I will say this, though," Reba continued. "If I was her, I never would have let anyone talk me into doing some televised press conference, because it's really no one's business, and the last thing I would want is for people to know my identity. I definitely wouldn't want people harassing me."

"Huh!" Melvin D spurted out. "For all we know, she wanted everyone to know who she was. For all we know, she couldn't wait to rub her husband's face in the whole thing, because as we all saw on television, he certainly didn't know she was the winner. You could tell from the look on his face and by all the stuff he said that she set up that media blitz straight behind his back."

"Oh my God!" Kennedi yelled out. "Why are they doing this?"

"Okay, I think that's enough about Mr. and Mrs. Mega Millions," J Sampson interrupted. "Plus, we need to find out how traffic is doing."

Kennedi switched the station and pressed on her brakes. Cars were slowing down more and more as traffic built up.

"What she probably did was check her numbers and then told him she wanted a divorce," another talk show host on a different station declared. "She probably put him out on the street in a matter of seconds."

Kennedi felt like crying. She'd had no idea things would get this bad, and now she wondered if she'd have to move to another state. Of course, with all the media coverage, people would probably still recognize her, but somehow she had a feeling it wouldn't be as unbearable.

When her Treo rang, she checked to see who it was and then pressed the button on her earpiece.

It was Patrice. "I hope you weren't just listening to J Sampson and the Morning Crew."

"Sad to say, I was, and can you believe the way they were criticizing me? Can you believe Melvin D had the nerve to insinuate that I was probably having an affair when I'm the one who's now a nervous wreck because it'll be two full days before I have my test results?"

"Girl, don't even pay those fools the slightest bit of attention. This is what they do every morning, and regardless of what they say about you, it's only a matter of time before everyone realizes Blake is the real villain in all this."

"But still, you know just as well as I do that some people believe everything they hear, and you can bet the rumors are already becoming more and more outrageous by the minute."

"That might be true, but eventually your story will become old news, and these people will move on to someone else."

"This is crazy."

"I know, but it'll pass. Maybe not as soon as you'd like for it to, but this will all settle down at some point."

Kennedi sighed but didn't say anything.

"So, after we hung up last night, did you hear anything else from Blake?"

"No, and I'm glad I didn't."

"I still can't believe he was at the house waiting for you when you got home."

"Neither could I, but now I know he's willing to do anything if he thinks he can get me to fork over fifteen million dollars."

"He's too much. I mean, how in the world could he even think he deserves two dollars when he's been sleeping with another woman all this time?"

"I don't know, but if he says he's going to fight for half, then that's exactly what he means."

"Then let him. Let him fight as much as he wants to."

"Yeah, but I can't help wondering if I'm really going to have to give him what he's asking for, and this morning I was even thinking that maybe it might be best to just make him an offer. Maybe he'd be willing to take a much smaller amount, so we won't have to spend unnecessary time in court."

"I say fight him until the end."

"But what if I lose?"

"You won't. Not once the judge finds out that he's an adulterer and that he moved out and sent you divorce papers before he even knew about the money."

"I don't think it's going to be that simple, because the law is the law."

"What you need to do is talk to Attorney Newman again."

"I am. I have an appointment with Miles this afternoon to go over a few things, but now I'm thinking I should call Attorney Newman to see if he has some time this morning for me to come in."

"That's what I would do."

Kennedi glanced at the screen on her cell phone. "Hey, let me give you a call back, because this is the security company calling. They're trying to schedule a time to install my new system."

"Talk to you later."

So, if you were me," Kennedi said after Attorney Newman closed his door and sat behind his desk, "what would you do?"

"This is a tough one. My first thought is that we should

gather as much information against Blake as we can and then let a judge decide. But if we get a judge who believes all marital property should be divided equally, regardless of what the situation is, then we're in trouble."

"Do you think we should offer him something up front?"

"That might not be a bad idea, but not right away. For now, I'd rather we wait until you actually have the check in hand and then wait to see what Blake's next move will be."

"He'll never back down. Not under any circumstances."

"Maybe he'll embezzle some money from his employer or commit some other serious crime," Attorney Newman joked. "Then, once he's caught and sent to prison, you won't have a thing to worry about."

Kennedi smiled. "That would be perfect."

"I know you want this to be over, but I say let's not do a thing until we hear from his lawyer."

"Whatever you say, I'm fine with, and thanks again for seeing me on such short notice."

"It's not a problem. Call anytime. You have my home and cell numbers, too, so please don't be afraid to use them. Day or night."

Kennedi stood up. "I won't."

Then she left his office and headed to work.

Chapter 12

It was three o'clock, and after arriving in her office two hours late and then leaving two hours early to meet with Miles, Kennedi might as well have taken off the entire day. Since it was Friday, though, and she only had less than a couple of weeks to go, she decided it wouldn't have been a good idea.

"Right now," Miles pointed out while leaning forward against the conference room table, "you still have twelve million to work with. You're investing fifteen and tithing three of it, but you haven't outlined what you want to do with the rest."

"Well, I'd like to set aside at least another five for spending and possibly some additional money for investing, and then use the other seven for gifts and donations."

"Sounds fine to me, but you need to decide how much you're giving to each individual. Remember, you were supposed to get that information to me by Monday." He smiled.

"I know, I know. And then I was planning to get it to you

yesterday after the press conference, but after the big Blake fiasco, well . . ."

"I'm really sorry that all that had to happen."

"Well, it's not like it's your fault."

"No, but I just hate seeing you go through all this public scrutiny when you don't deserve one tiny bit of it."

"It's tough, but it's not like I have a choice, and all I can hope is that this works out in my favor."

"I hope so, too."

"For now, though, let's count on giving one million dollars each to my aunt Lucy, my aunt Rose, and to Patrice. Then I was thinking two hundred thousand to each of my four cousins and two hundred to my in-laws together. Of course, if it turns out that I have to give fifteen to Blake, then we'll have to divide everything by two."

"Got it. But for our purposes, we'll base everything on the entire thirty, and with that being the case, you still have three million left of the seven. That is, minus the hundred thousand you want to give to the breast cancer foundation you mentioned last week."

"There's a shelter for abused women and children that I want to give a hundred to as well, and I also want to set aside maybe eight hundred thousand so that I can create a scholarship fund for underprivileged senior girls who've maintained at least a three-point-o average in high school."

"That's a great idea. A really wonderful one."

"I've always wanted to do something like that, and now I finally have the chance."

"Well, that leaves two million."

"I haven't quite decided what other organization I'd like to give something to, so let me think about it," she replied, but suddenly thought about her impending test results and how regardless of whether they came back positive or negative, she wanted to contribute toward AIDS research. She couldn't deny that she hadn't thought much about donating in that area in the past, but now she realized firsthand just how important it was.

"Are you sure five million is going to be enough for you to do some things for yourself?"

"*More* than enough."

"Well, if you change your mind, your investments will be bringing in more than enough additional income, year after year."

"I'll be fine."

"Then I guess all we have to do now is sit back and wait for your check to arrive."

"Yeah, that and the outcome of the court proceedings. Something I'm definitely not looking forward to."

Kennedi leaned back in the oversized tub that she and Blake had purchased a couple of years ago when they'd had the master bathroom remodeled and closed her eyes. She'd been sitting and relaxing, enjoying the hot, soothing bubbles for easily thirty minutes, and she didn't want it to end. The water felt amazing and the cinnamon bubbles smelled luscious. She'd even lit candles and placed five of them perfectly around the border of the tub, and had dimmed the lights shortly thereafter.

She sat there, savoring every moment, and before long, she started daydreaming. She'd never been a reckless spender, and even as a child, she'd been very practical, but she'd be lying if she said she hadn't thought about the kind of house she wanted to live in. She'd be lying if she said she wanted an existing home when she knew full well she wanted nothing less than something built from the ground up. She wanted a five-bedroom house with three finished levels, two staircases, a huge formal dining room, a massive living room with sky-high ceilings and gigantic picture windows, and marble flooring installed inside the vast entryway. She wanted a kitchen that would measure four times the size of the one she had now and a deck that would comfortably hold no fewer than twenty-five people at one time. She wanted to purchase all of her patio furniture from that Frontgate catalog, the one she'd been receiving for years but had never even considered actually ordering from. She wanted to choose her appliances, countertops, flooring, and everything else without having to worry about the cost of it. She wanted to hire a reputable interior designer to help with all her furnishing decisions and purchase one of those pure-white 735 BMWs she sometimes saw others driving around town in.

But as soon as Kennedi finished her last thought, she felt guilty. Uneasy. Selfish, even. Because somehow it just didn't seem right, her focusing on ridiculously expensive luxuries when there were so many people who didn't have food to eat. There were single mothers and elderly people on fixed incomes who struggled monthly, trying to figure out how to make ends meet, yet here she was fantasizing about millions of dollars she hadn't even worked for.

Kennedi opened her eyes and then closed them again, but after a few minutes, the phone startled her. She'd brought it into the bathroom, just in case it rang, but now she was sorry she had, because she didn't want to be interrupted.

She grabbed her towel, dried her hands, and reached out and picked up the cordless from the floor.

"Now what?" She groaned when she saw that it was Blake calling. "Hello?"

"Kennedi?" the female voice tried to confirm.

"Yes, who is this?"

"Serena, and if it's okay, I'd like to talk to you."

"Excuse me? Talk about what?"

"Blake and how you know he's entitled to fifty percent of those winnings."

"We must have a bad connection."

"No, you heard me correctly. And I'm dead serious, because I think it would be best for everyone if you stopped holding this grudge and just give Blake his share. It would be easier if you do it without being forced."

Kennedi raised her eyebrows and laughed, but then grew stern. "If you want to live, you'd better make this your last time calling here."

"Look, sweetheart, don't be mad at me just because the best woman won. Because maybe if you'd been taking care of Blake the way he needed to be taken care of, he'd still be over there with you."

"You can save that crap for somebody who cares, because, honey, I don't want him. You and Blake can have each other. And for the record, you can let him know that I'd rather see him six feet under before I give him ten pennies of that money. I'd rather see both of you murdered in cold blood," Kennedi said, and flung the phone against the bathroom wall, wishing instead that she could have cracked Serena across her face with it.

• • •

Kennedi got out of the tub, moisturized her body, and slipped into a beautiful satin nightgown. She'd been saving it for a special occasion and as a surprise for Blake, but as of today, she no longer needed a reason to wear nice things. She no longer needed a reason to pamper herself or a man to justify it.

She sat back on three pillows and spooned out a helping of the vanilla custard she'd picked up on the way home. Then she turned on the television and saw a rerun of Jamie Foxx's sitcom. It was the last episode of the series, the one where he and Fancy finally got married. She'd seen it several times over the last few years and she'd even shed a few tears each time she heard Jamie singing to Fancy, but today, all Jamie did was piss her off. Today she saw him the way she now saw Blake, the man who had pretended to love and honor her, the man who had stood beside her at a church altar and lied before two hundred and fifty witnesses.

So she turned the television to a local news show instead and stopped when she saw a clip from her press conference. They only showed her segment briefly and then immediately switched to the part that showed Blake entering the room.

Kennedi wished all this madness would stop. She wished they would find something else to obsess about so they could leave her and Blake's debacle alone. As it was, last night they'd played clip after clip, over and over, and now they were doing the same thing again. It was as if they didn't have anything else to run, and Kennedi wasn't going to watch any more of it. That is, until she heard one of the evening anchors saying they'd taped an interview with Blake Mason earlier this evening and would now play an excerpt.

"So, Mr. Mason," the meticulously made-up and very well-dressed anchorwoman started. "Is it true that you knew nothing about your wife having the winning ticket until yesterday morning?"

"Yes, that's correct. And I have to tell you, I was stunned. I never would have imagined her being the type of person who would try to get over on me the way she's trying to do. I never would have guessed that she would try to deny me what is rightly mine."

"Have you spoken with her? Tried to come to some sort of an agreement?"

"Yes, but she doesn't want to hear anything I have to say, and she's made it pretty clear that she's not giving me, in her words, ten pennies."

"You got that right," Kennedi told the television.

"I'm sorry. I didn't mean to upset you," she said when she saw a lone tear drop from Blake's left eye.

"No, don't be. This isn't your fault, and I guess I'm just so hurt because I never thought my wife would betray me this way, and it just goes to show that you really don't know who people are, not even the people you're married to."

"If you don't mind me asking one last question, are you going to seek legal action?"

"Absolutely. And I'm planning to fight this thing for as long as I have to. Years, if that's what it takes."

"Thank you for talking to us, Mr. Mason, and of course we wish you all the best."

"Thank you for caring enough to have me on."

Kennedi didn't know whether to throw up or applaud Blake's Academy Award–worthy performance. But what she did know was that she was going to pay him back for everything he'd done to her in the past and for the way he was now trying to make her out to be the troublemaker. He was such an innocent victim, to hear him tell it, but that façade would soon drop. She knew it wasn't right, throwing stone for stone, but Blake had crossed far too many lines. He'd crossed one after another, and Kennedi would never be able to rest until he'd gotten what he had coming to him. She wouldn't be satisfied until he suffered brutal consequences. The kind he would never forget.

Chapter 13

Four weeks had passed, but Kennedi was still tearfully thanking God a thousand times over, every single day, for protecting her the way He had. She'd called the eight hundred number, entered an anonymous code, and received the wonderful news—she'd learned that she was HIV-free. Of course, she would have to test again in about six months and then again one year from now to be safe, but nonetheless, she felt a major sense of relief. Then, if that wasn't blessing enough, the infamous check had finally arrived. Not five, not ten or even twenty, but more than thirty million dollars.

Kennedi had carefully examined the rectangular slip of paper on and off ever since picking it up yesterday afternoon from the lottery office, but no matter how many times she looked at it, the whole idea of it seemed insane. It was simply ludicrous, and she knew it would be a long time before she truly accepted the reality of it all. She was also sorry that because of terrible traffic conditions, she hadn't made it back to her bank before closing and had been forced to bring the check home with her. She had securely locked it in her safe, and yes, her security company had installed a pretty high-tech system with television monitors and other equipment, but she wouldn't feel at ease until it was out of her hands for good.

Kennedi placed the draft back inside its envelope and smiled when she spotted the huge plant, the one her coworkers had presented her with two weeks ago. They'd thrown her a huge party on her last day at work, and she was never going to forget it. Everyone had been so nice to her and had blessed her with such amazing gifts, and even now, she was almost in tears again. She'd never felt more special and more appreciated, and while she hadn't fully figured out how she'd go about doing it, she would thank all of them in a very memorable way.

After finishing the final touches of her makeup, Kennedi slipped on a pair of white, wedge-heeled sandals, which matched perfectly with her summer white pants and white sleeveless top, and headed out to her car. The sun shone brightly, and now she knew the Weather Channel had given a very accurate forecast: no clouds and a high temperature near eighty-five. Although this wasn't all that unusual for the last week in June, and she hoped the conditions would remain the same for the Fourth of July, which was only eight days from now. Aunt Rose had invited her over along with the rest of the family members who resided in the area, and Kennedi was really looking forward to spending time with everyone.

As she drove into her bank's parking lot, she saw Miles waiting inside his vehicle and pulled up next to him. They both smiled and stepped outside at the same time.

"Thanks again for coming," she told him. "I don't think there will be any problems, but I wanted you here just in case."

"I'm glad to do it," he responded, and they walked through the glass double doors.

Inside, Kennedi proceeded toward the teller line and Miles followed suit. They waited for only a minute or two and then the next available representative smiled. "Can I help you?"

Kennedi and Miles walked over and Kennedi pulled out the check, endorsed it, and then passed it over along with the deposit slip she'd filled out that morning, right after getting up. "I need to add this to my checking account."

The woman gazed at her cheerfully, trying to keep her composure, and Kennedi could tell she knew who she was. She hadn't even looked at the actual amount yet, but she seemed noticeably excited.

"Oh my goodness," she exclaimed quietly.

"That was my reaction, too," Kennedi said, and they all chuckled.

"Well, I guess all I need is to see your I.D. I mean, of course I know it's you, but I still have to follow policy. Sorry."

Kennedi handed over her driver's license. "It's no problem at all, and actually, I'm glad you're doing what you're supposed to."

"I'm glad you understand. I have to check the signature card you have on file with us, but it shouldn't take more than a couple of minutes."

"Sounds good," Kennedi said, and the woman hurried away.

"You're not about to pass out or anything, are you?" Miles teased.

"No. At least I don't think I am."

"I'll bet this whole thing still feels like some weird dream, though."

"It does. No matter how much I know it isn't."

Kennedi and Miles stood at the counter for ten minutes, and Kennedi started to get worried. She didn't want to think the worst, but she hoped Blake hadn't done something crazy like file a cease-and-desist order. Last week, Attorney Newman had warned her that this might happen, but since she hadn't heard from Blake, not since the night that Serena had found the nerve to call her, she'd assumed he was going to wait to handle this money situation during their divorce proceedings. But now she wasn't so sure, because she couldn't imagine it taking this long to match signatures and make a deposit. Yes, it was an unusually large sum of money, but as far as she knew, basic transaction procedures should have been the same for any amount.

Kennedi turned to Miles. "It sure is taking a long time."

"I was thinking the same thing. She's been in that back room for a while."

Kennedi felt her nerves stirring, took a deep breath, and folded her arms.

Miles rested his hand against her back. "It'll be fine."

Kennedi glanced over at him but said nothing, because at present, she thought otherwise. She tried to think positively, but she couldn't stop herself from remembering her last conversation with Blake and how adamant he'd been about taking her to court and suing her for not part, but all of her winnings. He wouldn't dare. Or would he? Would he actually be low enough to try and take everything from her and then share it with that tramp he was shacking up with?

Kennedi cringed, but just as she did, the teller returned.

"I'm so sorry it took this long. There was a glitch in our system, and we couldn't pull up your information. Plus, I shouldn't be saying this," she admitted now in a whisper, "but my supervisor wanted us to make sure we hadn't received any legal orders, I guess from your husband, and I'm happy to say there weren't any."

Kennedi felt relieved. "I understand."

"I do need to make you aware of one thing, though," the woman continued. "Because of the amount, we'll have to place a five-day hold on your deposit, and since today is Tuesday, funds won't be available until next Tuesday. I know that seems like seven days instead, but it's only because we don't count Saturdays and Sundays. I hope this won't be a problem for you."

"Not at all. I figured you would need to make sure the check cleared."

"Well, then, here's your receipt, and thank you so much for your business. Oh, and just so you know, we do offer private banking for our elite customers, and we can have someone contact you regarding investments and other products."

"Thanks," Kennedi agreed. "That'll be fine." Penelope was already handling her major investments, but she was still planning to keep checking and savings accounts at this particular bank for her everyday needs and monthly bill payments. Some of them, anyway.

When they went back out to their cars, Kennedi grinned at Miles and hugged him without thinking. "Thank you for everything," she said, and then took a step back.

"You're quite welcome."

"I don't know what your schedule is, but if you're open, I'd like to take you to lunch. Patrice had an important meeting with her top client that couldn't be changed, but I really feel like celebrating."

"I'm free as a bird. Just tell me where, and I'm there. Or we could drive together if you want."

A few weeks ago, Kennedi would have never considered riding in the same vehicle with Miles or any other man she hardly knew, but today she felt comfortable with him and wanted to be in his company.

"I can leave my car here," she proposed. "That is, if you don't mind dropping me back later on to pick it up."

"That works for me."

"Then let's go."

Morton's was one of Kennedi's favorite steak restaurants, and she was glad Miles had suggested it. As it had turned out, though, they'd arrived downtown about an hour before it had opened for business and had ended up strolling along the Magnificent Mile. Then they'd headed over to the East Wacker Place location and walked inside.

They didn't have a reservation, but thankfully, they were seated pretty quickly.

Kennedi hung her handbag across the corner of her chair. "I love this restaurant."

"I do, too. Come here all the time. Especially when I'm taking out potential clients."

"It has a great atmosphere, and the food is wonderful."

"I like the one in Schaumburg as well."

"Blake and I—" She stopped herself. "I've gone to that one a few times myself, and it was just as good as this location."

"That's going to take you a while."

"What's that?"

"Being able to go days and weeks without mentioning something you and your husband did together."

"I didn't mean to bring his name up."

"After ten years, I don't think you can help it. No one could."

Another waiter poured ice water into each of their glasses, and seconds later, their assigned waiter took their wine and salad orders, but they declined any appetizers. Then, since they already knew what they wanted, he wrote down their entrée choices.

When the rather frail twentysomething young man walked away, Kennedi said, "I guess I should have inquired about this before now, but it is okay for us to be having lunch, isn't it?"

"Of course. And why do you ask?"

"I wasn't sure if you were seeing anyone or not, and the last thing I want is to cause any problems. I know our relationship is strictly business, but there can still be a very fine line when it comes to people of the opposite sex spending time together."

"Trust me. You're not. I mean, I have been dating someone for about a year, but over the last couple of months, we've been slowly drifting apart."

"I'm sorry to hear that."

"Don't be. It's been coming for a while. We do still talk on the phone, but we barely see each other once a week."

"That bad, huh?"

"She's just not who I thought she was. I liked her a lot, but the more I saw how terribly she speaks to her mother and how often she neglects her six-year-old daughter, I started to lose all respect for her. Sometimes she leaves her daughter with her mother for weeks at a time, and it's not because she's working late or has other responsibilities. She does it because she doesn't want to be bothered."

Kennedi lifted her water glass. "That's too bad, and you have to wonder why women like that even have children."

"I know, but unfortunately, you see it all the time."

"I never wanted that responsibility for myself, but I do love children and I hate hearing about people who don't treat them the way they should be treated."

"That's because you have a kind heart, but some people only care about themselves."

The waiter sat both of their salads on the table, and as they picked up their forks, Miles paused. "I hope this isn't out of line, but do you think you'll ever trust another man again?"

"It's not out of line at all, because I've been thinking about that a lot."

"I'm sure."

"And the answer is, I don't know. But if I do, it will be a long time from now. I trusted Blake completely and I'll regret it for the rest of my life."

"I can imagine. But I will say that not every man is untrustworthy. Take me, for instance." He smiled. "I've always been a one-woman man."

Kennedi raised her eyebrows and then continued eating her salad.

"I know it's probably hard for you to believe, but being faithful and loyal is very important to me."

"That's good."

Miles laughed. "I'm glad you sound so convinced."

"I'm sorry, but I can't help it."

Miles pulled a card from the inside of his suit jacket and passed it over to her.

Kennedi took the snow-white linen napkin and patted the corners of her mouth. "What's this?"

"Just a little note."

She opened the envelope with her name on it and pulled out a small card, which read: "To a woman who deserves every blessing imaginable. Know that I couldn't be happier for you, and that I appreciate the amazing opportunity you have given me in terms of handling your financial affairs. Your best interests will always be my priority, both personally and professionally."

Kennedi reread every word. Not because she hadn't understood them the first time around, but because she wasn't ready to look into his eyes. She was so moved by all that he'd written and could no longer deny her attraction to him. But sadly, her connection to him would never be any more than what it was, because she refused to be hurt again.

"So, is he the reason you're trying to beat me out of my part of the money?" Blake yelled, and Kennedi jumped like a child. She'd been so consumed with her thoughts, she hadn't noticed him approaching the table. "You've got everyone thinking you're so, so innocent, when you've obviously been sleeping around behind my back all along."

Kennedi was at a loss for words but finally said, "What are you talking about?"

"You know exactly what I'm talking about. We're still married, yet you're out here advertising your new man to everybody."

By now all heads were turned toward them, and Kennedi wanted to disappear. Into thin air.

"Look, man," Miles interrupted. "Your wife is a client of mine, and all we're doing is having lunch."

"Was I talking to you?"

"No, but you're making a scene, and you're doing it for no reason."

"I think you'd better mind your own business," Blake instructed, and then turned his attention back to Kennedi. "You still think you're slick, but I know you've already deposited that check because I was sitting across the street from your bank when you went inside. I have friends all over this city, so no matter what you do, I'll always end up hearing about it."

"Blake, this is not the place for this."

"Oh, really? But it was the right place that day you showed up at the eatery near our house and caused all that commotion."

Miles stood up and dropped a few twenties on the table. "Kennedi, I think we should go."

Blake frowned. "You've got to be kidding. This is *my* wife, and if I want to talk to her that's exactly what I'm going to do. You, on the other hand, can leave anytime you get ready."

Kennedi rose from her chair. "Blake, just stop it."

"I only came here to give you one last chance to do the right thing. Once last chance to come to your senses."

"Good-bye, Blake," she said, and she and Miles walked toward the entry. Customers were chattering a mile a minute and Kennedi couldn't wait to get out of there. But as soon as they stepped outside, Blake confronted them all over again.

"I'm warning you, Kennedi. Do the right thing or else."

"Don't say anything," Miles told her.

"You know, I'm getting real sick and tired of you telling my wife what she should and shouldn't do. You're acting like you're the one who's married to her, and that can only be for one reason. She's already been giving it up to you. She's probably been giving it to you for years like some whore. Either that or you're just sniffing around, trying to see how much money you can get."

Miles turned around and faced Blake. "You're taking this too far, and if I were you, I'd stop while I was ahead."

"What?" Blake frowned and then raised back his fist and swung it forward.

But Miles blocked it and punched Blake in his jaw.

Blake grabbed the side of his face. "You're going to jail."

Miles shook his head. "Man, not only are you pitiful, you're pathetic."

Kennedi grabbed Miles's arm. "Let's go. Please."

Miles did what he was told, and strangely enough, Blake didn't follow behind them.

But in the car, Miles apologized. "I'm really sorry. I never should have let him get to me like that, but when he called you a whore, I lost it."

"No, I'm the one who's sorry, because Blake had no business confronting us. He had no business following us or saying anything at all."

"He might be upset about the money, but I think the idea of seeing you with someone else was the real issue. At least today, anyway."

"I don't know why. Not when he's living with someone else."

"I'm just telling you. The look in his eyes practically screamed jealousy."

"This is crazy, and that's why I'll be so glad when this divorce is final."

Miles drove out of the stall and through the parking garage, and suddenly Kennedi remembered what Blake had said, that he knew she'd deposited her lottery check, and she wondered how. She'd only told Patrice, Attorney Newman, both of her aunts, and of course, Miles, but once again, someone had betrayed her confidence. She had no idea who it could be, but after this, she knew she had to be a lot more careful. She had to be a lot more cautious regarding her business affairs and with safeguarding information she didn't want Blake knowing about.

It was time for her to realize she simply couldn't trust everyone. Maybe not even Patrice or her own flesh and blood.

Maybe not even the man she was sitting in the car with.

Chapter 14

Girl, it was a straight-up disaster." Kennedi had just gotten home from picking up her car at the bank and was on the phone with Patrice, telling her about the restaurant fiasco.

"I can't believe he flipped out like that."

"Neither can I, but then again, I can't believe any of what he's been doing. As of late, you never know what Blake might do. The man is full of surprises, and it's hard to believe I was married to him all this time but really didn't know him."

"But in all honesty, do we truly know anyone? I'm talking completely."

"I used to think it was possible, but not anymore. Not after the way Blake's been acting—and then I didn't tell you that someone told him I'd gotten the check. Which means someone told something I asked them not to."

"Who knew about it? Because you know I would never repeat any of your business. I haven't even told my mother about it."

"You, my aunts, Attorney Newman, and Miles."

"But you don't think your aunts would deceive you, do you?"

"I don't want to, but who's to say? And I definitely don't want to point the finger at Miles or Attorney Newman, because they know everything I'm doing and they're representing everything I have, legally and financially. But it's not like I've known Miles for all that long. He seems okay, but you never know. Then I can't totally dismiss Attorney Newman, because Blake and I do have a history with him, and how do I know Blake isn't paying him for information? For all I know, he might be trying to convince Attorney Newman to mishandle my case so he can win his."

"Gosh, I hope not."

"I don't know. Maybe I'm just paranoid."

"Maybe. But the thing is, someone is talking more than they're supposed to be, so being careful is very smart."

Kennedi didn't say anything to Patrice's last comment, but the more she listened to her best friend in the world, the guiltier she felt. She hated suspecting the people she cared about and prayed that she'd find the real culprit soon enough. Nonetheless, she knew for sure Patrice was telling the truth. Kennedi knew she would never hurt her under any circumstances. She knew it with all her heart, and that gave her so much peace.

Patrice continued. "When money comes into play, mothers will backstab daughters and vice versa, and it's a terrible shame."

"It is, but I knew when I won that certain people were going to act differently toward me or feel as though I owe them something. It's just the way it is."

"Well, I don't expect anything."

"Please. You *know* you're getting something. As soon as this Blake situation is settled."

"I'm just saying, though. I loved you like a sister before the money, and I still feel the same way now that you have it. Nothing's changed as far as our relationship is concerned. Period."

"I love you, too, Patrice."

They chatted a while longer, mostly about Patrice's wedding and how Kennedi wanted her to choose any gown she wanted, the best wedding planner, and the best reception site. Then they talked about everything and nothing for a whole other hour, the same as always.

But no sooner than when they'd hung up, the doorbell rang. Kennedi wasn't expecting anyone and wondered who it was. When she arrived at the door she looked out and saw her two cousins, Aunt Rose's two sons, Raymond and Joseph. She didn't mind them visiting, but the least they could've done—the least anyone could do—was call before simply dropping in.

She opened the door and looked up, because they both stood at least six foot two or six foot three inches tall. "What are you two doing here?"

"Hey, cuz," Raymond said. "We just so happened to be in the neighborhood and thought we'd stop by to see how you were."

There was a chance he was telling the truth, but Kennedi seriously doubted it. Still, she went along with his story.

"Well, that was nice of both of you."

"Yeah, cuz," Joseph added. "We thought we'd come check you out. See how things are going now that you're living like the Rockefellers."

Kennedi led them into the family room. "I don't think so, because as you can see, I'm still living the same as usual. This is the same house I've been residing in for the last few years."

Raymond plopped down on the sofa. "That might be true, but it's only a matter of time before you're on to much bigger and much better things."

Kennedi changed the subject. "So, how's Aunt Rose?"

Joseph rested his right ankle on top of his left knee the way men sometimes do. "She's good."

"I talked to her for a few minutes yesterday, but I haven't had a real conversation with her in over a week," Kennedi stated. "I'll have to call her back tonight or tomorrow."

"She'll be glad to hear from you," Raymond said. "No doubt."

Joseph looked around the room. "I see you still like elephants, huh?"

"Yeah, I guess so."

"I remember when we were little and you liked them even back then. The only difference now is that the ones you've got here are a lot more expensive than those plastic ones your mom used to buy for you when you were just a small girl."

"You've got a great memory," she complimented him.

"I know."

"We used to have such a good time back then," Raymond chimed in. "I know we were only cousins, but we grew up the same as any brothers and sisters would. We were at each others' houses all the time. You, Lisa, Bell, and us."

Lisa and Bell were Aunt Lucy's two daughters, both of whom had gone to college in Texas, had become successful nurse practitioners, and had decided to make their homes in Dallas. Kennedi was so proud of both of them, and when they'd called her a few weeks ago on a three-way call, she'd been extremely happy to hear from them. They'd laughed for what seemed more than two hours, and it had felt like old times. So much so that they'd each pulled out their calendars and scheduled a full spa weekend in Florida for just the three of them in late October.

"Yep, we were together all the time," Kennedi agreed. "And a lot of it had to do with the fact that our mothers were basically inseparable. They were so very close to each other, and I loved that about them."

Joseph rubbed his beard. "So did I."

"Me, too," Raymond said, and then Kennedi offered her two cousins something to eat. It was only leftover pizza from the night before, but they seemed thrilled and unable to get enough of it. She was actually having a great time with them—until their conversation swerved in a different direction.

Raymond wiped his hands with a paper towel and said, "Now, cuz, you know I wouldn't ask if it wasn't important."

"Ask what?"

"If you can let me hold twenty-five hundred dollars."

This was another one of those wow-I-just-don't-know-what-to-say moments, so Kennedi just listened.

"You see, the thing is, the engine in my Cadillac needs to be replaced."

If Kennedi's memory served her correctly, that was the same 1990 Cadillac that had been out of commission and backed into Aunt Rose's garage for more than a year, and she couldn't help wondering why he hadn't seen a need to get it fixed before now. Of course, forty-five-year-old Raymond had always been on the lazy side—Joseph, too, for that matter—and no job meant no money. However, today he'd somehow decided his "cuz" could easily pick up the tab for him.

Kennedi tried but couldn't resist asking him exactly what she was thinking, almost word for word. "Hasn't that Cadillac of yours been out of commission and backed into Aunt Rose's garage for more than a year now?"

"Uh, yeah, but, uh, you know, uh, you know how it is," he stammered. "You know how it is, cuz. It's rough out here. Work is basically nonexistent."

Not at McDonald's, Burger King, or Wendy's, was what she wanted to say, but she didn't want to argue with him or have him thinking she was suddenly talking down to him because of her newfound wealth. That wasn't her intention, but she knew Raymond would claim that she was for all eternity, and Joseph would quickly second his motion.

He continued before she could respond. "The reason I need my ride is because I can't look for a decent job without one."

Kennedi cracked up inside but then broke the bad news to him. "I wish I could, but so far I don't have access to any of my lottery money yet."

Kennedi was sort of leading him to believe she hadn't received the check at all, but in reality, she was telling the truth, because the money really was on hold until next week.

"Well, when will you?"

"What? Have the money?"

"Yeah."

"Soon, I hope."

"Then it shouldn't be a problem, because I know you have twenty-five hundred in the bank even without that jackpot."

Kennedi didn't like Raymond's tone or the sly look on Joseph's face. "I'm sorry, but I can't do it. Not right now."

Joseph got up from the island and laughed. "Okay, now, cuz, please don't tell me you're already gettin' the big head. Don't tell me you're about to forget who your family is. The people you share the same blood with."

At first, Kennedi was shocked that Joseph would say something so offensive, but then she thought about the fact that Joseph was worse than Raymond. The man was forty-two and had five children out in Philadelphia that he never bothered taking care of. He did work on occasion, at least a lot more often than his brother, but he was a veteran deadbeat father. Although, not too long ago, Kennedi had heard from her aunt Rose that Child Support Enforcement had finally caught up with him and that he had a court date in the near future.

"I'm sorry," she reiterated.

Raymond drank the last of his soda and threw the can across the tabletop. "Yeah, I bet you are. Man, let's go," he said to Joseph. "Let's get out of here before Miss Thing kicks us out or calls the cops on us."

"I don't believe both of you are acting like this. Over money."

"No," Joseph said as they headed toward the front door. "*We* don't believe you're acting like this. All high and mighty and like you're better than us."

"She sort of always acted that way anyhow," Raymond explained, and spoke as if Kennedi wasn't in the room with them. "Way before now, and especially ever since she married that no-good Blake. I never liked that little uppity attitude of his in the first place, and now that joker got the nerve to be going on television acting all innocent when Mom was saying how he's the one who's sleeping with another woman."

Joseph followed his brother outside. "I know, man, but for all we know, dude might have had good reason to do what he did. Maybe his situation at home wasn't up to standard, if you know what I mean."

Kennedi slammed the door behind them, and while she'd originally planned on giving each of them two hundred thousand dollars, after this, she wasn't so sure. After this, she wasn't sure they deserved anything from her, and while she hadn't sworn her aunt Rose to secrecy when it came to Blake's affair or his leaving her, she wasn't happy to know that Aunt Rose and her lowlife sons had been thoroughly discussing it. Probably joking about it and saying how naïve Kennedi had been. Probably criticizing her the way they criticized every other family member, both in their faces as well as behind their backs. Hmmph. Maybe Aunt Rose's million needed to drop to a mere five figures—fifty thousand at the most. Maybe what Kennedi needed to do was reevaluate that entire household so she could figure out who genuinely cared about her. Not just when there were special circumstances, but unconditionally.

Chapter 15

Kennedi flipped through the day's mail but stopped when she came across a large square envelope that displayed a return address she didn't recognize; however, the sender's name was extremely familiar: Nina Cole. Kennedi's best friend from kindergarten and the girl who'd remained her favorite person all the way through third grade. But then Nina's father's employer had transferred him to one of their western locations in Arizona, and Kennedi and Nina had slowly but surely lost touch with each other. They'd spoken on the phone several times for maybe the first twelve months or so, but after that, they hadn't communicated much at all, and eventually Kennedi had found a new best friend named Patrice to play with. She could only assume that Nina had probably done the same.

Kennedi pulled out the beautiful card adorned in soft pink and lavender and took a seat in the kitchen. She couldn't wait to read what her childhood friend had written and wasted not another second.

> *KK,*
>
> *Surprise! I can't believe it's been just over thirty-one years since we last saw each other, but after seeing you all over the media, I couldn't let another day go by without saying congratulations and telling you how happy I am for you. I was so excited when I realized it was you who'd won the Mega Millions jackpot—you, the first best friend I ever had.*
>
> *I tried calling you, but when I checked with directory assistance, they informed me that your number was unlisted, so I figured I would drop you a few lines by mail. Strangely enough, I was still able to get your address from an online phone book, so I hope you don't mind me contacting you. And of course, if you find that you have some time to chat, please call me. I would love to hear from you, and my number is written below.*
>
> *Well, I won't hold you, but again, know that I am elated for you and that I pray all of God's continued blessings upon you.*
>
> *Nina*

Kennedi smiled. What a truly pleasant surprise this was, and even though it was near ten P.M., she reached for the phone and dialed Nina's number. It rang twice and then Nina picked up.

"Hello?"

"Miss Cole?" Kennedi sang.

"KK?" Nina said, referring to the nickname she'd given Kennedi back when they were five and only hours after they'd met. She obviously had caller I.D.

"Yes, it's me."

"Oh my goodness. It's so good to hear your voice. How are you?"

"Wonderful. I certainly can't complain."

"I guess not."

"So, what have you been doing all these years, and what area code did I call? Are you still in Arizona?"

"Yes. I live in a suburb just outside of Phoenix."

"Have you been there the entire time?"

"All except the four years I was in D.C. attending Howard."

"Amazing."

"What about you? Have you always been in the Chicago area?"

"Pretty much, but I did go away to school down at Illinois State."

"How are your parents?"

"They both passed away."

"Oh, I'm so sorry to hear that."

"Thank you. What about yours?"

"They're both doing very well. I just stopped by to see them about an hour ago, and they'll be so excited to know I got a chance to talk to you."

"I'm excited myself. Your card really made my day."

"So, do you have any children?"

"No. I decided right out of high school that I didn't want any, and I've never changed my mind."

"Nothing wrong with that," she said and then changed the subject. "So, you know I have to ask. What in heaven's name are you going to do with all that money you won? The whole thing is just so awesome."

"I know. For the first few weeks, it didn't seem real, but now it's sort of sinking in."

"I can't even imagine."

"So, do you have any children?"

"Yes, two sons, ten and twelve, but I'm divorced from their father."

"Well, I'm sure you've heard about my marital situation, too."

"Unfortunately, I have, and I really think it's a shame how these people keep discussing your business on national television. What they need to do is get a life."

"It's the one thing about winning the money that I don't like, because being in the public eye was never something I wanted to experience."

"I know what you mean, and I hope it will pass in due time."

Kennedi switched the phone from one ear to the other. "So do I."

"So, have you figured out how much you're giving to all your friends and family members?"

Kennedi scrunched her face. What kind of question was that, and why was Nina asking her this? "I've been thinking about it, but I won't be able to finalize anything until the situation with my husband is taken care of."

"Oh, that's right. Well, I will tell you that I've been testifying to people out here on a daily basis, because as soon as I saw you on television, I knew God had answered my prayers. For two years, I've been trying to figure out how I can come up with fifty thousand dollars to open a barbecue restaurant, and when

I heard you say you were giving money to your family members and friends, I broke into tears. I bawled like a baby, because I knew God was speaking to me as clear as day."

Kennedi wanted to say something, but she couldn't make any words come out of her mouth. Was Nina serious? Did she actually think she was entitled to fifty thousand dollars? Simply because they'd been friends some thirty-plus years ago? She couldn't. There was no way.

"God is so miraculous!" Nina continued. "He's so true to His Word, and I have no idea what I would do without Him. To think He chose my best friend to help me. I've dreamed about opening my own business for years, and finally, it's all coming together."

"Nina, I think maybe there's been some sort of misunderstanding."

"I don't get what you mean."

"About the money you're talking about. The money you claim God wants me to give you."

"There's no misunderstanding at all." Her tone had changed the same way that Raymond's had a few hours ago. For the worse.

"Maybe it's just best for me to tell you straight out. I can't loan you fifty thousand dollars."

"I never said anything about a loan, because God told me that you were going to *give* me what I needed."

"That's fine, but there's one problem with that."

"What?"

"Well, if God really and truly wanted me to do this, don't you think He would have told me the same thing He told you?"

"I'm sure He did, and maybe you're just ignoring it."

"No. I would never do that. I always try to do the right thing, and I always try to help anyone who legitimately needs to be helped."

"So what are you saying? That I'm lying?"

"No. But what I am saying is that God hasn't spoken to my heart about any of this. Not once."

"Well, you know what? You do whatever you feel you have to do, but don't blame me when it comes time for you to answer to Him. Don't call me when you're being punished because of your disobedience."

"Excuse me?"

"That's right. Because when you don't do what God tells you to do, you have to suffer the consequences. When you don't help your fellow man or woman, you'll be judged for that in the end."

"I think it's time for me to hang up now."

"Fine. But just remember, money is the root of all evil, so if I were you, I'd try to get rid of some of it before you end up in hell."

"No, the Bible says the *love* of money is the root of all evil, and trust me when I tell you, I've never been obsessed with money, not even now."

"Is that why you're hoarding it from your husband and why you're refusing to share his part of it with him?"

"No, that's not it at all. And even though none of this is any of your business, he doesn't deserve it, because he left me for another woman and slept with her for years unprotected."

"Whatever."

"Whatever is right," Kennedi repeated, and hung up.

Was this ever going to stop? People thinking she owed them

something? Was this whole money thing going to cause her to lose friendships with everyone she'd ever made acquaintance with? Because it wasn't like she could give every single person she knew any amount they asked for. Yes, thirty million dollars was a lot of money, but she couldn't hand out money to every Sally, Jane, and Henry just for the sake of doing so. As it was, she didn't know if she would even have the full amount by the time Blake finished suing her. And why was Nina using God as a way to get what she wanted, anyway? Not to mention, if she was such a true Christian, how could she have possibly taken on such a nasty attitude toward the end of their conversation? How could she have gone from being overly friendly to sounding like a longtime enemy in a matter of minutes?

Kennedi dropped the card and the envelope inside the trash bin and opened the refrigerator. She pulled out a bottle of water and then took a glass from the cupboard and filled it with ice cubes. But just then, the doorbell rang. She was in her night-gown already and didn't have on a robe, but she went to the door to see who it could be, especially at this hour.

"Who is it?"

"Me."

"Blake?"

"Yeah. Baby, I need to talk to you."

"No. Haven't you done enough?"

"Kennedi, please. I'm sorry about the way I acted earlier, but I really need to talk to you."

"Blake, no. And if you don't leave, I'm calling the police."

"Kennedi, I promise this won't take long, and I've even decided that I'm not taking you to court. So please let me in. Baby, this is really important."

She didn't know what to do, but she had to admit that she was curious to know why he had all of a sudden changed his mind regarding legal action.

"Kennedi, please."

She sighed, opened the door, and hoped she wouldn't regret doing so.

He crossed the threshold and Kennedi turned away and headed into the family room.

"Why did you get the locks changed?" he wanted to know.

"Because I didn't want you coming in here whenever you felt like it."

Blake sat on the love seat, adjacent to where Kennedi was sitting on the sofa. "You look good. As beautiful as ever."

"Blake, what do you want?"

"Well, first of all . . . I really messed up."

"And you think that's new information?"

"No, but I can't go on like this, and it's time I acknowledged what I've done to you."

Kennedi crossed her arms and stared at him.

Blake continued. "Over the last few weeks, I know I've said some pretty harsh things to you, but I didn't mean any of it. Not one word, and I was also lying when I said I no longer loved you."

Kennedi pursed her lips. "Is that right?"

"Yes, and the only reason I moved out and filed for a divorce was because I didn't see where I had any other choice."

"And what do you mean by that?"

Blake hung his head backward and covered his face with both hands. Then he smoothed them down his cheeks and looked at her. "I had to do it, because Serena was pregnant with twins. But then she had a miscarriage."

If Kennedi hadn't known better, she would have sworn this wasn't Blake at all and that instead, some other madman was sitting across from her, rattling off a load of untruths. She'd have sworn the man positioned in front of her wasn't able to distinguish what was real and what wasn't, and that he desperately needed psychiatric help.

"Did you hear me?" he asked. "I said Serena was pregnant."

"You're way too much for me," she said. "Amazing."

"I never meant for anything like this to happen. Actually, I never meant for any of it to happen, but one thing led to another, and the next thing I knew, I was seeing her on a regular basis and I couldn't stop."

"No, what you mean is you *didn't* stop."

Blake looked defeated. "I'm sorry. I know my words don't mean much at this point, but I'm really, really sorry. And I want you to know that the only reason I've been so cold and so cruel to you is because it helped me believe I didn't want you anymore. It made it a lot easier for me to leave you. It was almost as if I was playing head games with myself. I knew I loved you, but at the same time I can't deny the fact that I didn't want my children growing up without me. I felt the only proper thing to do was marry their mother, but now I know I was wrong. I know I was wrong for hurting you, and I never should have left."

"And you're telling me this because?"

"I'm sorry. I'm pouring my heart out to you because I made the biggest mistake in my life, and I don't want to lose you. I don't want a divorce, and I want to make everything up to you."

Kennedi wanted to strangle him. Or worse. But she tried to calm herself before speaking. She tried to forget about the tabloids and how they were going to have a field day with this baby saga if they ever found out about it. "It's too late for any of what you're talking about, and all I want is for you to leave me alone. For good."

Blake got up, came over to her, and dropped down on his knees. "Kennedi, please don't throw away ten whole years. I know I was wrong, but everybody makes mistakes. I was wrong, but when I saw you with another man this afternoon, it tore me apart. It hurt me in a way I can't even explain."

"And how in the world do you think I feel?" she yelled while pushing him away and standing up. "How in the world do you think I've felt ever since you walked out of here? Huh?"

"I know, and I'm sorry."

"Blake, how many times are you going to say that?"

"Well, what can I do to make this right?"

"Nothing. It's as simple as that."

"Kennedi, please. I'll spend the rest of my life doing whatever you want me to do. If you tell me to jump, the only thing I'll want to know is how high and for how long."

"What you mean is that you'll do whatever you have to in order to get your hands on that lottery money."

"No, that's not it, because my attorney has pretty much assured me that I'll be awarded no less than one half of everything."

"Then as far as I'm concerned there's nothing else to talk about."

"Would it help if I told you that I don't love Serena? Because I don't. I thought I could, but now I know it will never happen."

"And so are you thinking that if I take you back, we can suddenly live happily ever after like two newlyweds? Because if you are, I have news for you. I'm not Charlotte Black."

"You're not who?"

"Blake, never mind. Just get out."

"Kennedi, if you'll only think about all we've been through."

"You mean like the two-year affair you've been having with Serena, all while still sleeping with me at the same time?"

Blake didn't say anything, and that defeated look overtook him again.

Kennedi walked out of the family room.

"Where are you going?"

"To show you out once and for all."

At the front door, Blake caressed the side of her face. "I still love you, and I'm not giving up."

Kennedi turned her head away from him, and he finally left.

She closed the door and couldn't help fixating on Serena and the fact that the woman had almost had a baby with *her* husband. Twins, to be exact.

But more important, she still wondered why Blake was all of a sudden being so remorseful. She wondered why he'd suddenly had such a major change of heart.

She wondered what could possibly make him change his mind about taking her to court and why he was shamelessly begging her to take him back.

There had to be a reason, and Kennedi couldn't wait to find out what it was.

Chapter 16

Patrice stretched her legs all the way in front of her and said, "Can you believe we're actually sitting inside this humongous limousine, heading downtown to shop on Michigan Avenue?"

Kennedi laughed at her and then gazed out of her window. It certainly was a dream come true, the two of them, best friends for life, preparing to shop for as long as they wanted and without any preset spending limits. As promised by the teller one week ago, Kennedi's funds were now available, and Kennedi had decided it was time she and Patrice went out and enjoyed themselves. Of course, she wouldn't do this on a regular basis, because one only needed so many pieces of clothing, shoes, and jewelry, but today they were going to purchase their hearts' desires. Today they would live like Hollywood celebrities and not feel bad about it.

"So, did Blake call again this morning?" Patrice asked.

"Yep. Right on schedule at eight o'clock."

"My goodness, when is he finally going to give it a rest?"

"I don't know. He's called every day since that night he came over, and I didn't get to tell you that yesterday afternoon, he sent me another dozen roses."

"Isn't that the third time?"

"Mmm-hmm."

"How pitiful. I mean, does he actually think you're going to just forget everything he's done to you?"

"Actually, I think he does. He's been pleading tirelessly, and he won't stop."

"And all because he wants you back?"

"That's what he says, but you know, I think there's more to it. Especially since he changed his mind about suing me."

"Whenever something seems a little far-fetched, my grandfather used to say, there's a dead cat on the line somewhere. Now, I'll admit, I have no idea what that means, but I think that theory definitely applies to Blake."

"I do, too, but eventually he'll get the message, and maybe when he does, he'll leave me alone," Kennedi added, and then saw the privacy window sliding open.

"I'm sorry to interrupt you ladies," the driver said while looking at them in the rearview mirror. "But here we are."

They pulled in front of the Louis Vuitton store, and while Kennedi had seen it and passed by it on plenty of occasions, she'd never actually gone inside, and now she knew there really was a first time for everything.

"This is just too much," Patrice declared.

Randy, the driver, opened Kennedi's car door, which was closest to the curb, and they both slid out of the limo. "I'm going to drive over a couple of blocks, but here's my cell number so you can call me when you're ready."

"Thanks, Randy. And actually, I should warn you that it's probably going to be a little while."

He smiled. "I figured as much, and it's not a problem. Waiting is what I do, and I'll probably just get a bite to eat and do some reading."

Kennedi repositioned her black leather handbag farther across her right shoulder. "Sounds good. See you later."

Patrice waved her hand at him. "Yeah, see ya."

"You ladies have a great time."

Inside the store and to the left stood a cheerful-looking female security guard who greeted them right away. Next they were approached by a saleswoman.

"Hello, I'm Susan. How can I help you ladies today?"

"We're interested in seeing some of your handbags."

"Certainly. Did you have something in particular in mind?"

Kennedi moved closer to the glass case that the woman stepped behind. "Actually, yes, I was searching your site online, and since I love big purses, the Multipli-cité bag really caught my eye."

"Excellent choice," she acknowledged, and slid open the glass cabinet and pulled it out.

Kennedi sat her own bag on the counter and picked up the Louis Vuitton. "This is nice."

"It's definitely you," Patrice commented. "All the way."

"You think?"

"I do. Seriously."

Kennedi switched it from hand to hand and arm to arm, testing it out in the mirror. "I know this is the first one I've tried, but I don't think I have to look any further."

"It's very classy," Susan offered. "And as your friend said, it's very you."

"I'll take it."

"Wonderful. And what about you?" Susan asked Patrice.

"I've been sort of standing here admiring that one." She pointed.

"Oh, the Alma bag. That's another great choice. One of our classics."

Patrice waited for Susan to retrieve it. "I've always loved this whenever I've seen other women carrying it."

"I think it'll always be pretty popular."

Patrice stood in front of the same mirror Kennedi had just walked away from and slid the two short handles over her arm and down toward her elbow. "I've been wanting one of these for as long as I can remember."

"Well, now you can finally get one." Kennedi beamed, because the elated look on Patrice's face was priceless, and nothing made her feel better than being able to do something special for others, specifically for the people she loved and cared so deeply about.

Patrice examined the bag inside out and then looked at Kennedi. "Are you sure?"

"Positive. I told you this morning. Get whatever you want."

"Then I'll take it," Patrice confirmed.

Susan subtly eased the tote from Patrice, picked up the one Kennedi had chosen, and returned what must have been two floor models back where she'd gotten them. "You're really blessed to have such a good friend."

"I know," Patrice agreed.

"We're both blessed to have each other," Kennedi added.

"Well, before I head to the back to pull two brand-new bags, can I show you anything else? Maybe a couple of wallets?"

Kennedi stepped closer to the case again. "That would be fine."

"There are so many to choose from," Patrice pointed out.

"So many indeed," Susan said. "And it pretty much depends on how much space you need for money and credit cards."

Kennedi raised her eyebrows. "I can tell you right now that I need the largest one you carry."

"Isn't that the truth?" Patrice laughed. "And even that might not be big enough with all the stuff she totes around. She's always prepared for everything."

Susan chuckled along with her and then suggested six different styles before Kennedi and Patrice each chose the one that zipped all the way around and was roomy enough for just about everything, including a checkbook and pen. Then Kennedi decided she also wanted the Drouot, a shoulder bag that had a strap long enough to cross over her body, and Patrice chose the Portfolio for business. After that, they waited for Susan to wrap up their selections and bring them out to the checkout area, where Kennedi passed over her American Express Platinum Card and paid for them.

Then they strolled quickly across the street with two sizable dark brown shopping bags in hand and headed toward Tiffany. Kennedi had always wanted to purchase something that could be placed in one of those cute little blue boxes adorned with shiny white ribbon, and now she would finally have her chance.

But just as they stepped in front of the doorway, Kennedi's phone rang, and she decided to answer it before going inside.

Patrice waited beside her. Kennedi rolled her eyes in irritation when she saw that it was Blake.

"I'm ending this once and for all," she said to Patrice, and then pressed the answer icon on her Treo. "Hello?"

"Hey," he said. "How are you?"

"Fine."

"I tried calling you at home again, but I guess you're out."

"I am. So, is there something you wanted?"

"Just to talk to you."

"Blake, look. These phone calls have to stop."

"Why?"

"Because there's nothing else left for us to say. The court date for our divorce has been set for September, and that's that."

Blake totally ignored what she'd just said. "What are you doing tomorrow for the Fourth?"

"Going over to my aunt Rose's, but what does that matter to you?"

"I was thinking you could spend the holiday with me."

"Then I guess you haven't heard a word I've said, have you?"

"No, because no matter what you say, Kennedi, I love you, and I want you back."

"And I keep telling you it's not going to happen. And I mean that. I've never meant anything more, and I really wish you would leave me alone."

"It's that jerk you were with at the restaurant, isn't it?"

"Good-bye, Blake."

"I knew you were giving it up to him, because if you weren't, you wouldn't be acting so cocky and like you don't need me. You'd be jumping at the chance to have me back, regardless of what I've done."

Kennedi shook her head disgustedly, and she could tell Patrice wanted to know what he was saying.

"What if I am sleeping with him, Blake?" she said. "Because you and I both know that if I am, I'd be well within my rights, now wouldn't I?"

"Are you?"

"As a matter of fact I am!" She lied just to aggravate him. "I've been sleeping with Miles for months now, and you can't hold a tiny candle to him when it comes to sex. Happy?"

"I'm more than happy. You think you're so smart, but thank you, Kennedi. Thank you for being naïve enough to think I really wanted you back and for giving me all the ammunition I need," he boasted. And he hung up.

Kennedi dropped her phone inside her purse and groaned. "This won't be over soon enough."

"What was he talking about?" Patrice asked, opening the door and walking in.

Kennedi followed behind. "Girl, who knows? First he was begging, and then his whole attitude changed."

"I heard what you said about Miles. You crack me up!"

"You know I only said it to piss him off."

"Yeah, but it was still funny."

"Maybe now Blake will finally move on. Although I am wondering what he meant when he said I'd just given him all the ammunition he needed."

"He said that?"

"Yeah."

"Well, I wouldn't worry about it."

"You're right. I'm not about to let him ruin our day."

They walked up to a counter that housed ridiculously large

diamonds and left with blank stares when the salesperson told them the smallest one in that particular case was fifty-two thousand dollars. Kennedi now had millions, but the idea of spending that much money on any single piece of jewelry was senseless. Foolish, even. And it was something she would never consider doing.

But what she did do was purchase a stunning diamond-and-white-gold cross, a diamond-and-white-gold ring, a pair of three-carat princess-cut diamond earrings, and a couple of high-quality, sterling silver jewelry pieces that unquestionably met the .925 standard. Patrice followed up with a diamond-and-white-gold necklace and a pair of two-carat diamond earrings, even though Kennedi had made it clear she was welcome to get the same size she had.

Then, before leaving, Kennedi had purchased Miles a bottle of Tiffany for Men Sport cologne and a silver pen and letter opener for Attorney Newman as a thank-you for their services. Although she couldn't deny that her gift to Miles was a bit more personal than it was business. She also couldn't deny that since that day they'd gone to lunch, she hadn't been able to stop thinking about him. She, of course, was afraid to confess her true feelings to him, or even to Patrice for that matter, but deep down she liked him. She liked him a lot, and she didn't know what to do about it. Although she knew seeing him wasn't even an option until her divorce was final.

Over the next four hours, Kennedi and Patrice dipped in and out of stores and snapped up items from Saks, Neiman's, Victoria's Secret, and a few others—so much so that they'd had to ask Randy to bring the car around so they could pile all of their bags inside the trunk. They'd purchased everything from Lucky jeans to Manolo Blahnik shoes to a couple of Armani skirt suits and pant suits, but this was it. They'd enjoyed themselves in the most magnificent way, spending thousands, but now it was time to put the brakes on. It was time to get back to the logical way of spending Kennedi had always been accustomed to.

Kennedi sat inside the limo. "Randy, can you swing us back by the John Hancock building?"

"Sure," he said, and closed her door.

Patrice leaned back against the headrest. "Whew. Talk about shopping until you drop."

"That we did."

"But thank you, Kennedi. Thank you for everything."

"You know that's not necessary. I had a blast, and there's no one else I would have rather done this with."

"I'll never forget it. Going in stores I've only browsed in and then actually buying whatever I wanted? It's a dream come true."

"I'm glad you had a good time."

"I had a *sensational* time."

When Randy pulled up in front of the restaurant, Kennedi and Patrice got out.

"You guys are funny," he said. "You can afford to eat at any restaurant you want, but here you are getting ready to go inside the Cheesecake Factory."

They all laughed and Kennedi said, "I know, but the thing is, we love it. We'll always love it, and there's no cheesecake in the world like their pineapple upside-down cheesecake."

"I guess there's nothing wrong with that."

"Do you want us to bring you out something?"

"No, I'm fine."

"Okay, then, we'll be ready in a couple of hours, and I promise this is the last stop."

"Enjoy."

"He's such a nice guy," Patrice said as they walked inside.

"He is, and I'm going to make all of this worth his while when we get home."

"Didn't you already include the gratuity on your credit card when you reserved the car?"

"Yeah, but he deserves more than that. He's been so patient and so at ease, and I really appreciate that."

"This is true."

Kennedi heard her phone ringing and sighed. "Now what?"

"I'll check to see how long the wait is," Patrice offered.

Kennedi's face softened when she saw that the person calling was Attorney Newman.

"Kennedi? Did I catch you at a bad time?"

"No," she told him, and stepped back outside. "How are you?"

"Well, I was good until I received a call from Blake's attorney. Just got off the phone with him, and apparently your other half has changed his mind again."

Kennedi had told Attorney Newman about Blake's trying to reconcile with her, about Serena's pregnancy and the miscarriage, along with every other little detail she could think of, making sure Attorney Newman was up-to-date on anything that might help her case. "What did he say?"

"That Blake wants his full fifteen million, but he's willing to accept ten if you'll settle out of court and write him a check by this Friday, meaning three days from now."

"Why out of court and so soon?"

"I wanted to know the same thing, and maybe you can shed some light on what they're talking about, because Blake's attorney claims that Blake has taped information that will prove you've been having an affair behind his back and that it's been going on for a long time. He says if Blake has to, he's going to release it to the media."

"What?"

"That's what he said."

"He was actually taping our conversation?"

"So it's true? You told him that?"

"Yes . . . I mean, no. I mean, I told him, but only to upset him."

"But it's not true, though?"

"No. Absolutely not."

"I doubt it'll be admissible, but Blake's attorney is definitely going to do all that he can to bring it in as evidence, and you know how the media can spin certain stories in any direction they want to, and we wouldn't want a judge to be swayed one way or the other. At this point, all we'd have are your words against his."

"He was setting me up the entire time, and I should have never started talking to him."

"Well, what's done is done, and the fact still remains that he moved out of your house and in with another woman. The private investigator we hired has confirmed it."

"And will that help?"

"Maybe. But I won't lie to you. There is a chance Blake will win."

Kennedi heard what he was telling her, and all she could

hope was that Attorney Newman wasn't in cahoots with Blake and that he was really being on the up-and-up with her.

"My research assistant and I have been searching and searching for a case where the plaintiff walked away with nothing, but so far we haven't found one. What we did find were three cases where the plaintiff won, and in one situation, the plaintiff collected more than half the winnings because the judge felt like the husband shouldn't have had to fight for what was rightfully his."

Kennedi was saddened by all that Attorney Newman was telling her but finally said, "Can I think about it?"

"Yes, but I'm afraid you'll still need to decide by Friday if you want to take him up on the ten million."

"Do you think I should?"

"I don't want to suggest that, because I don't think Blake deserves a single dollar, but at the same time, paying him ten million will be a lot better than the whole fifteen. I was also thinking that it might be a good idea to call his attorney back with a counter-offer of seven and a half, just to see what happens, because it may be that Blake wants to make a deal and be done with this. Or we can go to court and take our chances. But I would say let's counter and go from there."

"Then maybe that's our best bet. The holiday is tomorrow, so can I call you on Thursday?"

"That would be fine, and if you don't get me, just try my cell."

"I will, and thanks for calling."

"No problem, and please try to have a good Fourth."

"You, too," Kennedi said, but had no idea how she'd be able

to enjoy anything, what with Blake practically guaranteed to get almost half the winnings after all.

She didn't know how she could enjoy tomorrow or any other day, knowing he'd taken up with some tramp, slept with her for two whole years whenever he felt like it, walked out on his wife, and was now getting ready to walk away with millions of dollars. Millions and millions of *her* money, and it just wasn't fair.

It wasn't right, but she had a feeling there wasn't a thing she could do about it.

Nothing except swallow her pride, write him a check, and get over it.

Chapter 17

K ennedi, baby, it's so good to see you." Aunt Rose beamed when Kennedi, Patrice, and Neil walked out to the back-yard. Patrice's parents were out of town visiting other relatives, and Neil's parents lived in Colorado, so they'd decided to celebrate Independence Day with Kennedi's family.

Kennedi hugged Aunt Rose and spoke loudly over the O'Jays, belting out none other than their astounding "Family Reunion." "The food smells wonderful."

"You know your cousin Lee Willie can grill his natural behind off and that James Michael," she said, referring to Lee Willie's brother, "can make the best barbecued baked beans in the country."

Patrice reached out and embraced Aunt Rose. "Thank you so much for having Neil and me over."

"Yes, thank you," Neil said.

"Glad to have you both. Wouldn't have had it any other way."

"Hey, sweetheart," Aunt Lucy said to Kennedi. "I see you made it. And hey, Miss Patrice. And Neil, I see you're still looking as handsome as ever."

"Isn't that the truth?" Aunt Rose laughed. "Just as fine as he wanna be."

"Ladies, please." He blushed.

They all chuckled.

But then Kennedi spotted Raymond and Joseph coming toward them with their ghetto-hoochie girlfriends in tow. They were already acting as if they didn't want to speak, and Kennedi hoped they weren't planning to act out part two of that show they'd put on over at her house one week ago.

At first they stared at her, but then Joseph broke the ice. "Good to see you, cuz."

"Good to see you, too," she said, and strangely enough, Joseph hugged her and then introduced her to his woman friend, Heineken.

"Like the beer?" Patrice noticeably couldn't help inquiring.

"Yep," the woman said. "My mama said she loved her some Heineken back in the day, and then she realized what a beautiful name it was for a little girl."

Kennedi was speechless, and so were Patrice and Neil; even Joseph seemed slightly embarrassed and didn't say anything. But to the side of them, Kennedi saw Raymond's girlfriend nudging his arm and him shaking his head in disagreement with whatever she was trying to get him to do.

"Then forget you," the woman finally said, and reached her hand out to Kennedi. "Hi, I'm Tarmisha. Your cousin Raymond is so rude, but it's a pleasure to meet you."

"It's a pleasure to meet you, too."

"You the one that won all that money, ain't you?"

By this time, Patrice couldn't take it anymore, and Kennedi watched her walk away, practically giggling like a teenager. Neil followed behind her, and Kennedi wished she could do the same thing.

But instead, she smiled at the woman, who looked much too young for Raymond. "Yeah, I guess that would be me."

"You got it goin' on. And if you need someone to help you around your house or do anything, all you have to do is call me," the woman said excitedly, and passed over what looked to be a phone number.

Not likely, Kennedi thought, but gracefully told her, "Thanks, and I'll let you know if something comes up."

Raymond rolled his red and very liquored-up eyes at her, and Kennedi knew he wanted nothing to do with her. He was still angry about the twenty-five hundred dollars she hadn't given him when they'd come over, and that was just fine with her.

Kennedi went around greeting all of her family members, close and extended, and she was happy to see Aunt Lucy's significant other and his two grown children. Aunt Lucy's husband had passed a few years back, and Kennedi was happy to see her with such a decent, caring man. She'd been dating Lyle for more than a year now, and Kennedi could tell Aunt Lucy was in love with him. She would never admit it, of course, mainly because she thought it was disrespecting her husband's memory, but Kennedi could tell she was more than fond of him.

Next, Kennedi strolled over to Lee Willie, her mother's first cousin, and saw him forking off a slab of ribs and placing it in a large pan. "Hey, Miss O." He beamed. "So, how's it goin'?"

"Good."

"Just good?"

"Well, actually, great."

"Now, that's more like it, and you know why I'm calling you Miss O, don't you?"

"No."

"Because as the young folks say, now you ballin' like Miss Oprah."

"Not exactly."

"But close enough."

Kennedi playfully flipped her hand at him.

"It's true, and while your ol' cousin likes to joke around, I'm serious when I say how happy I am for you and how proud I am to be related to you. I'm not saying that because I'm expecting any handout, I'm saying it because I mean it and because just between you and me, everybody out here in this backyard don't necessarily feel the same way. We got some jealous ol' people in this family, but no matter what anybody says, you just hold your head up and keep right on doin' what you doin'."

James Michael walked up behind his brother. "That's right. Don't pay none of these fools any attention, and don't let nobody make you feel bad about the way God has blessed you."

"Thank you. That means more than both of you realize, and the two of you can certainly look to hear from me in about a week or so."

Lee Willie grinned a wide grin and could barely contain himself. James Michael seemed just as thrilled as Lee Willie was.

Kennedi hadn't seen Lee Willie, James Michael, or any of her other second cousins in a long time, but she was definitely going to add them to the list of relatives she was giving gifts to, because they did seem genuinely happy for her.

After mingling for another half hour, someone turned down the music, Aunt Lucy said grace over the food, and they all got in line to eat. Kennedi looked down the three tables that were pushed together and covered with red, white, and blue tablecloths and knew she was about to indulge way more than she should. But how could she resist? There were ribs, chicken, brats, burgers, potato salad, baked beans, coleslaw, macaroni and cheese, green beans, and every dessert imaginable. The entire spread screamed hundreds of fat grams, carbohydrates, and calories, and Kennedi would have to work out a few minutes longer every day for the rest of this week just to make up for it.

As time passed, everyone ate, chatted, and cracked jokes, and Kennedi was glad to be in the presence of her family. They always knew how to have a good time, and Kennedi couldn't be happier.

But of course all good things must and do come to an end, and that's exactly what happened as soon as Raymond turned off the music and opened his mouth. Loudly.

"I want *you*," he demanded, pointing at Kennedi as he slurred his words, "and your little wannabe friends to get up from this table and get your little wannabe tails up outta here."

"Raymond, let's go inside," Aunt Rose yelled, obviously realizing how drunk he was and trying to put out a fire that was already well ignited.

"No! I want them outta here. I want them outta this backyard and in a hurry."

"Raymond, son, don't do this. Please, let's go in the house."

Raymond jerked away from her. "No, Mom. You know I'm right, because you were the one who told me that Kennedi thinks she's better than the rest of the family."

Kennedi heard gasps from every corner, and Aunt Rose seemed mortified. She was shocked that her own child had ratted her out, and he didn't stop there.

"Remember you told me that Kennedi had won the lottery and that you and Aunt Lucy were going to the press conference with her? And then I saw Blake at the gas station a few hours later, and he told me that he'd left Kennedi? Remember, Mom? Because that's when you said we shouldn't let on to Kennedi that we knew anything at all and that I should tell Blake about that lottery ticket. And then you also told me when Kennedi called you and said she'd finally gotten her check. Remember?"

"Raymond, you stop this right now! You stop telling all these lies on me."

"Lies? Mom, what's wrong with you? You scared of Miss Thing or something? Because you know I'm telling the truth. You were the main one saying how maybe if I told Blake everything that was going on, he would give us a nice reward from his cut of the money. Which is what I did. But then today, that no-good joker come calling me, talking about how my services are no longer needed and that he's not giving me another dime. He already paid me two thousand dollars, but that fool promised me a hundred thousand more if I gave him the four-one-one on what Miss Thing here was doing."

Aunt Rose gazed at her niece with pleading eyes. "Kennedi, baby, it just slipped. I was so excited for you that I let the stuff you told me slip, but I never told Raymond to tell Blake anything or cut any deal with him. I swear I didn't."

Raymond roared like he'd never heard anything funnier. "Mom, why don't you stop all this pretending?" he said, staggering backward. "This was all your idea, because you said for all you knew Kennedi might not give us anything and that Blake would be a good safety net."

Aunt Rose was angry but she seemed lost for words. "You're drunk."

"Maybe I am, but not too drunk to remember you saying how tight Kennedi was with money and how she got that crazy mentality from her mother."

Kennedi pushed away from the table. "*My mother?* Aunt Rose, you had the nerve to say something bad about my mother? Your own sister? Your sister who's not even here anymore?"

Aunt Lucy stood up. "Rose, you're wrong for this. Way wrong. And Kennedi, honey, I had no idea any of this was going on."

Kennedi grabbed her purse. "Patrice and Neil, let's go."

"Honey, wait." Aunt Lucy followed behind them. "Please don't let Rose or Raymond ruin your holiday. Don't let them steal your joy."

"I can't stay here, Aunt Lucy. Criticizing me is one thing, but saying bad things about my deceased mother, well, that's something different. Aunt Rose was always jealous of Mom, but it wasn't until today that I actually saw her for who she really is."

"I wish you wouldn't go, but I understand."

"I'll call you later," she said, and hugged Aunt Lucy.

"You take care."

Kennedi, Patrice, and Neil continued toward Neil's vehicle, but Kennedi heard Raymond shouting one obscenity after another and threatening to put a hit out on Blake for using him the way he had. Kennedi listened until she could no longer hear him and, without warning, sat in the backseat of the car and burst into tears. Why couldn't her mother be here for her? That way she wouldn't have had to tell either one of her aunts a single ounce of her business. Although she knew with all her heart that Aunt Lucy would never backstab her the way Aunt Rose and that lowdown Raymond had.

But believe it or not, there was a bit of good news that had evolved from all of this: Attorney Newman hadn't been the one supplying Blake with confidential information, meaning he hadn't been the one betraying her.

Even better, neither had Miles.

Chapter 18

Kennedi's eyes stretched wide open when the ringing phone snatched her from a deep sleep, but she grabbed it away from the nightstand by reflex. Thankfully, though, she'd looked at the caller I.D. screen before answering and sat it back down on its base. It was Aunt Rose and clearly the last person Kennedi wanted to talk to. She did love her mother's middle sister—how could she not?—but Aunt Rose had proven that she couldn't be trusted, and Kennedi knew it would be a long time before she saw or spoke to that woman again. The woman who, right after the press conference, had pretended she was so livid with Blake and who was so ready to give him a piece of her mind, when all along she was planning to swindle money from him and deceive Kennedi all at the same time.

However, when she picked up the phone to call Patrice, she saw the words "voice mail" and couldn't refrain from listening to the message.

"Kennedi, baby, I know it's early, but I'm just sick over all those lies Raymond told you. I haven't slept more than five minutes, and my nerves are just shot. I'm so sorry for all the pain Raymond caused you, and I really hope we can get past this. I'm hoping that you will realize how important family is, and that nothing is *more* important. Money is one thing, but in the end, our love for each other is what truly counts. I know Raymond was wrong for talking to you the way he did, and I was wrong for telling him the things I told him, but the thing is, people make mistakes. I'll forever be sorry, but sweetheart, your good old aunt isn't perfect, and I pray that you will find it in your heart to forgive me. I love you so much, and please call me as soon as you can."

Kennedi pressed three for delete and hung up the phone. It was amazing how Aunt Rose, after all that had happened, was still ready to lie for as long as she had to. Because there was no way Raymond, drunk or otherwise, would have falsified his mother's part in the whole Blake scenario. If Raymond said this was all her idea, one could take his claim to the bank. So why Aunt Rose was denying her involvement was beyond understanding, because Kennedi knew what the truth was. Aunt Rose was as guilty as sin and then some.

Kennedi stayed in bed for another twenty minutes, flipping through morning shows, but then finally called Patrice. Of course, the main topic of discussion was the big Fourth of July fiasco, but after that they talked about how much fun they'd had shopping on Michigan Avenue and . . . how much fun they'd had shopping on Michigan Avenue. Then, when they ended their conversation, Kennedi went down to the kitchen and had breakfast. She hadn't been to the grocery store yet this week, but she did find a cup of strawberry-banana yogurt, which she embellished with granola and a handful of grapes, and some low-carb apple juice to drink. When she finished eating and reading the *Chicago Tribune,* she threw a load of white clothing into the washer and then a group of colors inside the dryer and decided it was time to get dressed. She didn't feel like doing much today, but she needed to run a few errands before it got too late. As she started toward the stairway leading back up to her bedroom, though, the phone rang. She thought about ignoring it, especially since it was probably only her aunt again, but she was pleasantly surprised to see that it was Miles.

"Hello?"

"Hello yourself. So, how are you?"

"I'm well. And you?"

"Same here. So, did you have a good Fourth?"

"Not really. Actually, it was a disaster, but to be honest, I'd rather not talk about it."

"I'm sorry to hear that, and it makes me feel sort of bad, because I had a great time at my parents' house yesterday."

"Don't even think twice about that. It's not your fault that some of my family members are a bit dysfunctional."

Miles paused, obviously not knowing what else to say.

"So, what's new?" Kennedi asked.

"Not a lot. I've been thinking about you, and since I hadn't heard from you since that day we went to lunch, I figured I would give you a call."

"It's good hearing from you."

"I also wanted to talk to you about something if you have time."

"Go ahead."

"This might be a little awkward for you, but the truth is, Kennedi, I really like you a lot. I liked you from the first moment I saw you in Attorney Newman's office, and if you feel the same way, I'd like to start seeing you on a regular basis."

Kennedi wanted to respond, wanted to tell him she felt the same way, but she was too afraid of getting hurt. Too afraid to trust or have faith in him.

"You *are* still there, aren't you?" he said.

"Yes. I'm here, but I guess I don't know what to say."

"Why? Is it because you're not attracted to me?"

"No."

"Then what?"

"I don't want my heart broken again. I've been through so much over the last few weeks, enough to cover a lifetime, and I don't think I could handle any more disappointments."

"That's understandable, but believe me when I say I would never hurt you. I know you have no way of proving that, but I really care about you, and when it comes to hurting women, well, that's not who I am as a person."

"I just don't know, and even if I wanted to start spending time with you, I wouldn't be able to until my divorce is final."

"I understand that, too, and all I'm asking is that you give me a chance. That's all."

"I can't promise you anything, but I'll definitely think about it."

"I hope you're not hesitant because of what Blake said the other day."

"And what was that?"

"That I'm probably only hanging around because of all the money you have. But I assure you, your money has nothing to do with my feelings for you. As a matter of fact, I'll even sign a prenup if you want me to," he joked, and Kennedi couldn't help laughing.

"Oh, so now you've got us rushing down the aisle and getting married?" she commented.

"No, actually, I don't, but I was just trying to make a point. I'm trying to get you to see that I'll do whatever it takes to make you feel comfortable. And if it would make you feel even better, we can draw up a contract stating that I'm responsible for all dating expenses and that the only gifts that will be purchased are the ones I buy for you. Of course, if we end up falling in love or something like that, it would be nice if you at least got me a card for Valentine's Day."

"You're funny."

"Maybe, but I'm also very serious about being with you. And for the record, you and I both know that I have my own money, so using you for your money is certainly not my intention."

"I guess I can appreciate that."

"Okay, then for starters, can we at least have daily phone conversations?"

"I guess I don't see a problem with that."

"You're sure?"

"There's nothing wrong with talking, so I'm positive."

"Good. And I promise you, you won't be sorry."

"I really hope not, and just so we're on the same page, I think I should explain something to you up front."

"Explain away."

"It's really very simple. You know the saying 'Three strikes and you're out'?"

"Yeah."

"Well, all you get is one."

"Only one, huh?"

"Yep. So take it or leave it."

"Actually, my dear, I won't even need that. Not now, not ever."

Kennedi had finished running all her errands, but now that she was back home, she still couldn't contain the smile plastered across her face. She knew Miles might be full of it and that he'd probably only said what he thought she wanted to hear, but she had to admit that she was happy to have him in her life. Like a schoolgirl, she was already anticipating his daily phone calls and couldn't wait until she was finally able to go out with him in public. There was still a certain level of fear she would surely have to contend with, but deep down, she wanted to believe that Miles was worth it. She wanted to believe that not every man was like her soon-to-be ex, Blake Mason.

As soon as Kennedi completed her last thought, her cell phone rang. Her home phone had been ringing for what seemed all day long, and because her cell now displayed the word "private," she almost didn't answer it. But then she realized it might be Miles and hurried to press the button.

"Hello?"

"I assume your attorney relayed my message."

Kennedi felt her blood rushing. "And?"

"And I thought you should know that I'm not playing with you. If you don't settle this by tomorrow, I'm releasing the tape, and I think you'll be amazed at how advanced voice technology has become and how you might not even remember some of the things you actually said. If you force me, I'll end up being your worst nightmare."

Kennedi pressed the end button as hard as she could and dialed Attorney Newman.

"Kennedi? How are you?"

"Attorney Newman, enough is enough. I can't take this anymore, so let's just schedule a meeting for tomorrow and be done with this."

"Did something happen?"

"I just want this to be over," she practically demanded, but didn't mean to sound so rude.

"Okay, you're the boss, but do you at least want me to counter with the seven-point-five we talked about?"

"No. Let's just pay him what he wants. Let's end this before I end up doing something dreadful."

Chapter 19

Kennedi glared at Blake across the conference room table and wanted to leap on top of him. It had been almost twenty-four hours since he'd made that threatening phone call to her, but she was still as angry as ever. She was livid because he'd done exactly what he'd set out to do, win by unanimous decision, and it was hard accepting her defeat. It was hard meeting with him face-to-face and seeing how proud he was to have beaten her.

"I've taken the liberty of drawing up the appropriate documents, which outline the marital property agreement," Attorney Newman began. "I realize the reason we're here today is primarily because of Kennedi's lottery winnings, but I figured we might as well include everything so that we won't have to deal with any of this during the divorce proceedings. Attorney Green, do you have any objections to this?"

"No. My client and I concur, and actually we welcome your initiative in doing so."

"Then here are copies for both of you to review," he said, passing them over to Attorney Green. Kennedi already had her copy and was satisfied with all that was included, specifically the language that stated that Blake was forever barred from claiming any additional money from her.

Blake flipped through the pages pretty quickly, and it was obvious that he couldn't care less about their house, vehicles, bank accounts, or any other assets. It was clear that he cared only about his ten million and was ready to sign anytime they wanted him to.

"Everything looks to be in order," Attorney Green acknowledged. "Blake, do you agree?"

"Looks good to me."

If only Kennedi could do something bad to him and get away with it. Something he wouldn't soon forget. But she immediately said a quick prayer, asking God to free her from her evil thinking. She asked Him to free her from the violent thoughts she kept having and to cease the private movie now flickering through her mind—a movie starring Blake and Serena. A movie where the two of them were lying across a bed full of money and then laughing about how easy it had been for them to make such a fool of Kennedi.

So, yes, she prayed like never before and took a deep breath. She was glad this was almost over.

Attorney Newman passed over two pens, one to Kennedi and one to Blake, and they both signed on the lines they were instructed to. Then, Attorney Newman pulled out the envelope holding the cashier's check, the one Kennedi had gotten from the bank this morning, but was interrupted by a knock at the door.

"I'm sorry, Attorney Newman," one of the other secretaries apologized. "But you have a couple of visitors, and based on what they've told me, I think you'll want to see them."

"Now?"

"Right now."

"If you'll excuse me, I'll be right back."

Blake stood up. "Actually, if you'll just give me my check, I'll be on my way."

"Please don't do that, Attorney Newman," the secretary pleaded. "Please, just step out here, and I'll explain what the situation is."

"I'm sorry," Attorney Newman told Blake, and then looked at Attorney Green.

"This is a bunch of bull," Blake whined. "I have places to go and people to see, so I don't have time for all of this petty stuff."

Attorney Green relaxed farther into his chair. "Hopefully he'll be back shortly."

Blake scowled at Kennedi. "All I know is that this better not be some stunt you're trying to pull."

Kennedi stared at him but didn't say anything. She had not a clue what this interruption was all about, and while she'd never let on to Blake, she was just as curious about it as he was.

But all curiosity was satisfied in a matter of seconds.

"Hello, Blake." A statuesque, fortysomething woman stepped into the room, and Blake looked as though he'd just finished a Stephen King novel. He looked terrified, stunned out of his wits, and very trapped.

But the other shocker was the fact that Serena had walked in right behind her, and Kennedi could tell they'd come together. Attorney Newman told the first woman that the floor was all hers, and she wasted no time saying what she had to say. "I just couldn't go through with this, Blake."

"Katherine, what are you doing here?" he finally asked.

Serena squinted her eyes. "No, actually it's *me* you should be worried about, because I'm the one who brought her. I'm the one who you thought was too stupid to check up on you, but what you didn't know was that I figured out that password to your voice mail a long time ago. You changed it when you left Kennedi, but then I watched you type the new one in, too, and that's all I needed."

"Serena, please don't do this."

"Oh, I'm definitely doing this, because you deserve whatever you get. I loved you, Blake, and I'm carrying your twins, so how on earth could you do this to me?"

So, she really is pregnant, Kennedi thought. Blake had claimed that Serena had miscarried, but now Kennedi knew he'd only told her that because he'd been faking like he wanted her back and because he wanted her to believe he no longer had any obligations to Serena. This also explained why he'd suddenly wanted to settle so quickly and outside of court.

Attorney Green looked from person to person but didn't say anything. Attorney Newman seemed amused by all that was happening.

Serena turned to Kennedi. "I know you'll probably never forgive me, but I'm sorry. I'm sorry for sleeping with Blake and for getting pregnant by him, and if it's any consolation, I'm already getting my payback. Because, you see, this lowlife right here has been sleeping with Katherine and pretending like I don't even exist. But then after I listened to some of her messages, I called her and told her he was living with me and that we were expecting two babies. And can you believe he had the audacity to tell her that as soon as he got his part of the money, he wanted them to get back together?"

Kennedi raised her eyebrows. "Back together?"

"Oh," Serena continued. "Did I forget to tell you that they're married?"

"That's right," Katherine confirmed. "And Blake knows it."

"This is crazy!" he yelled. "All I want is my check so I can get out of here."

"I don't think so," Katherine objected. "You're married to me, remember? Not Kennedi."

"Why couldn't you have just died the way you were supposed to? The way I left you all those years ago?"

Katherine slowly shook her head from side to side, and it was obvious she hadn't expected Blake to make such a heartless statement.

Kennedi was shocked by his words as well, but she couldn't help wondering what the odds were of something like this happening. Winning the lottery *and* finding out your cheating husband was a bigamist. She guessed one in a million. Or more.

"Maybe you should explain," Attorney Newman told Katherine, and Katherine sang like Jennifer Holliday and Jennifer Hudson all wrapped up into one.

Apparently, Katherine had been watching the press conference and realized the husband of the winner was legally *her* husband—of twelve years. Blake had only been in his late twenties when he'd married her, but as fate would have it, Katherine had soon found out she'd been stricken with a rare blood disease. At first, the doctors had been hopeful, but eventually, they'd told her they'd done all they could do and that she had six months left at the most. Blake, however, hadn't coped with the news very well and had finally told Katherine that he could no longer deal with her illness. He'd hung around for maybe another week or so but then apologized and told her he was leaving the next day.

They'd been living in California, and since Katherine had been near death, she never bothered asking him where he was going. She'd decided that if he was cruel enough to leave her right when she was dying, then she wanted nothing else to do with him.

But, thank God, her disease had miraculously gone into remission and she'd been fine ever since. She'd admitted that it was crazy and irresponsible of her not to file for a divorce, but as it had turned out, one year had led to another, and after a while she'd no longer thought all that much about it. There were times when she had considered hiring a lawyer and filing papers, but like so many other men and women in the country, she just hadn't. She'd decided to live her life in California and to let Blake live wherever he was living, and that was that.

By now, Blake was beyond humiliation. "You make me sick," he said, glaring at Katherine and heading toward the doorway. "And you," he said, pointing at Serena. "As soon as I pack my stuff, you can forget about ever hearing from me again."

"Oh, I think I'll hear from you quite often. I'll be hearing from you every single week, once you start sending my child support payments."

Blake cracked up laughing. "You silly, silly woman. If you think I'm paying you as much as one nickel, you're even dumber than I thought you were."

"No, you're the dumb one, Blake. So dumb that you actually thought you could scheme your way into millions of dollars and then simply walk right out of here with it. But unfortunately for you, we fixed all of that, didn't we? We stopped you dead in your tracks, and there's not a thing you can do about it."

"You can say that again," Katherine added. "There's not a thing he can do except run out of here with his tail between his legs."

Blake tossed both of them a dirty look, flung the door open, and then left the conference room. His attorney followed behind him, and Kennedi asked Attorney Newman and his assistant if she could have a few minutes alone with Katherine and Serena.

"You know, not that it matters one way or another," Kennedi said to Katherine, "but how were you even able to contact Blake?"

"I found a listing for his parents and asked his mother if she would have him call me. I don't think they have a clue that Blake and I are still married, and I never told them differently. But his mother did give him my message, and he phoned me right away because I think he knew there was going to be trouble if he didn't get back to me."

"When did you first see him?" Kennedi wanted to know.

"He flew me in about three weeks ago, and I've been here ever since. I took an indefinite leave of absence from work."

"And you were willing to take him back even after he left you to die?"

Katherine chuckled. "You won't like what I'm about to say, but the only reason I came here and the only reason I slept with Blake was because I knew he was about to get paid. I knew that whether he kept his word about us getting back together or not, I was going to be rich. Either as his wife or as his blackmailer. It didn't matter to me one way or the other. But then I found out about Serena, and when she told me about those two little ones she was carrying, all I could think was how horrible it felt when Blake walked out on me and how he obviously didn't care about anyone. Then I thought about the fact that God had been merciful enough to spare my life all those years ago, yet here I was plotting to steal money from someone I didn't even know. I realized how wrong I was, and then Serena and I decided that Blake had to be stopped."

Kennedi sat there in a daze, not knowing how she should feel. On the one hand, she still despised Serena for sleeping with the man she thought was her husband, and to be honest, she wasn't all that happy with Katherine either. But on the other hand, she couldn't deny that these two women were the reason Blake had walked away with nothing. They were the reason Kennedi no longer had to worry about any divorce proceedings or Blake in general. It didn't seem real, but she was finally free of the man she'd never actually been married to in the first place and able to move on with her life.

Kennedi hadn't felt this good in a very long time and decided she was going to do something most women would never even consider.

"I won't lie," she told Katherine as she filled out a check. "I'm still not sure how I feel about you or about the fact that you were basically planning to steal from me, but what I do know is that Blake would have walked away with ten million dollars if you hadn't come forward. There is a chance that I still might have found out he was a bigamist, but you can bet I never would have gotten all of my money back. So this is for you."

Katherine looked at the draft and then back at Kennedi.

"After the terrible thing I was going to do, you're giving me a hundred and fifty thousand dollars?"

"I am. For services rendered," Kennedi said, and then stood and strolled toward the door."

Serena frowned. "Wait a minute. What about me?"

Kennedi glanced back at her. "You? You get absolutely nothing. Except maybe a hard way to go."

Chapter 20

No matter how many times I think about Blake already having a wife, I'll never be able to fathom it," Patrice said matter-of-factly.

"It's a real trip," Kennedi agreed. "No doubt about it, and I'm just glad he hasn't tried to contact me."

"That's because he's probably scared to death that you're going to press bigamy charges against him."

"You're probably right, but I'm through with Blake and everything that has to do with him. Ever since he walked out on me, all I could think about was paying him back—in the worst way possible—but now the only thing I want is to be at peace. All I want is to close this unfortunate chapter and move on with my life."

"I don't blame you, plus now you've got Miles, anyway."

"Yeah, right."

"Well, you do."

"For the time being."

"I think he's the one, Kennedi. I see the way he looks at you, and it makes me very happy."

"I hope you're right, but we'll see soon enough."

"I guess we will," Patrice said, and then went to answer the ringing doorbell.

It was Sunday afternoon, and Kennedi was glad some of her relatives were starting to arrive. She'd invited over Aunt Lucy; her second cousins Lee Willie and James Michael; and three other distant family members. She'd even considered letting bygones be bygones when it came to Aunt Rose, Raymond, and Joseph—especially Joseph, since he'd at least had the decency to speak to her at that holiday cookout—but she just wasn't ready to deal with such trifling individuals. Maybe she would feel better about the whole situation at some time in the future, but not now.

"Hi, sweetheart." Aunt Lucy smiled and embraced her niece.

Kennedi held her close and for longer than usual. "Hey, Auntie, I'm so glad you could make it."

"I know I've told you on the phone a couple of different times, but I can't apologize enough for Rose and Raymond's behavior on the Fourth of July. It was totally uncalled for, and you didn't deserve to be treated that way."

"Don't worry about it. And after what I just found out about Blake, that drama with the two of them is child's play."

"I guess so."

Over the next twenty minutes, everyone else filed in and took a seat around the family room, and Kennedi walked in front of the fireplace. "I'm sure most of you are wondering why

I called you here, but then again, you might have figured it out already. Anyway, now that my financial situation is settled, I wanted to get all of you together as soon as possible," she said, holding a stack of envelopes. "I wanted you to know that I love you and that I appreciate the way you've supported me and how you've been there for me my entire life. Unfortunately, Daddy was an only child, so the only real family I have is all of you who are from Mom's side, and I hope you know that I'll cherish each of you always."

Kennedi's eyes filled up and she blinked quickly, trying to prevent any tears from falling. But she couldn't. "This is from me to you," she continued, her voice shaky, while passing out each envelope one by one.

When Aunt Lucy opened hers, she squealed like a small child on Christmas Day and then rushed toward Kennedi, hugging her and thanking her profusely.

"You are more than welcome, and I already mailed Lisa and Bell something yesterday," Kennedi told her. Then she addressed the rest of the group. "I hope everyone understands that because Aunt Lucy is my mom's oldest sister and more like a mother to me, she got just a little more than the rest of you," Kennedi announced, referring to her aunt's one-million-dollar gift.

"Of course, we understand," Lee Willie replied. "Young lady, this two hundred thousand I got right here is more than enough."

"I know that's right," James Michael concurred. "This is more money than I know what to do with."

The others commented similarly, but when Kennedi looked over at Patrice and saw massive tears streaming down her face, she knew Patrice, like Aunt Lucy, had seen all seven figures.

Kennedi smiled and Patrice silently mouthed the words, "Thank you. I love you with all my heart."

Kennedi took a deep breath and couldn't remember the last time she'd felt so warm inside. Now she knew that no matter how much money a person held in his or her possession, it was so much better to give than it was to receive. It was so much more rewarding, and now that she thought about it, she'd had that same feeling when she'd given her tithe at church that morning. And she knew she would experience the same kind of happiness once again, tomorrow afternoon, right after Miles wrote checks to each of her designated charities.

She was glad God had placed her in a much better position to help others, and she wouldn't let Him down. She still wanted her dream house and she still wanted to enjoy life as a whole, but more than anything, she wanted to make a difference. She wanted to help those who were in need without any regret.

What she wanted was for her mother to be proud of her.